THE CAST

(Not in order of appearance)

Peanut: The dog

Grape: The cat (later, purple)

Bino: The mean dog

Fox: The smart dog

Rex: The big dog

Joey: The weird dog

Maxwell: The other cat

Sasha: The dumb dog

Daisy: The dumber dog

Fido: The suave dog

Sabrina: That one cat

Spo: The mouse

Spot (superdog): The fictional dog

Stripe: The fictional ~~cat~~ dog

Tiger: The dog???

Marvin: The other other cat

Zach: The bun-bun

Pete: The mythical superbeing

var. Humans: Themselves

Mr. Bigglesworth: Themselves

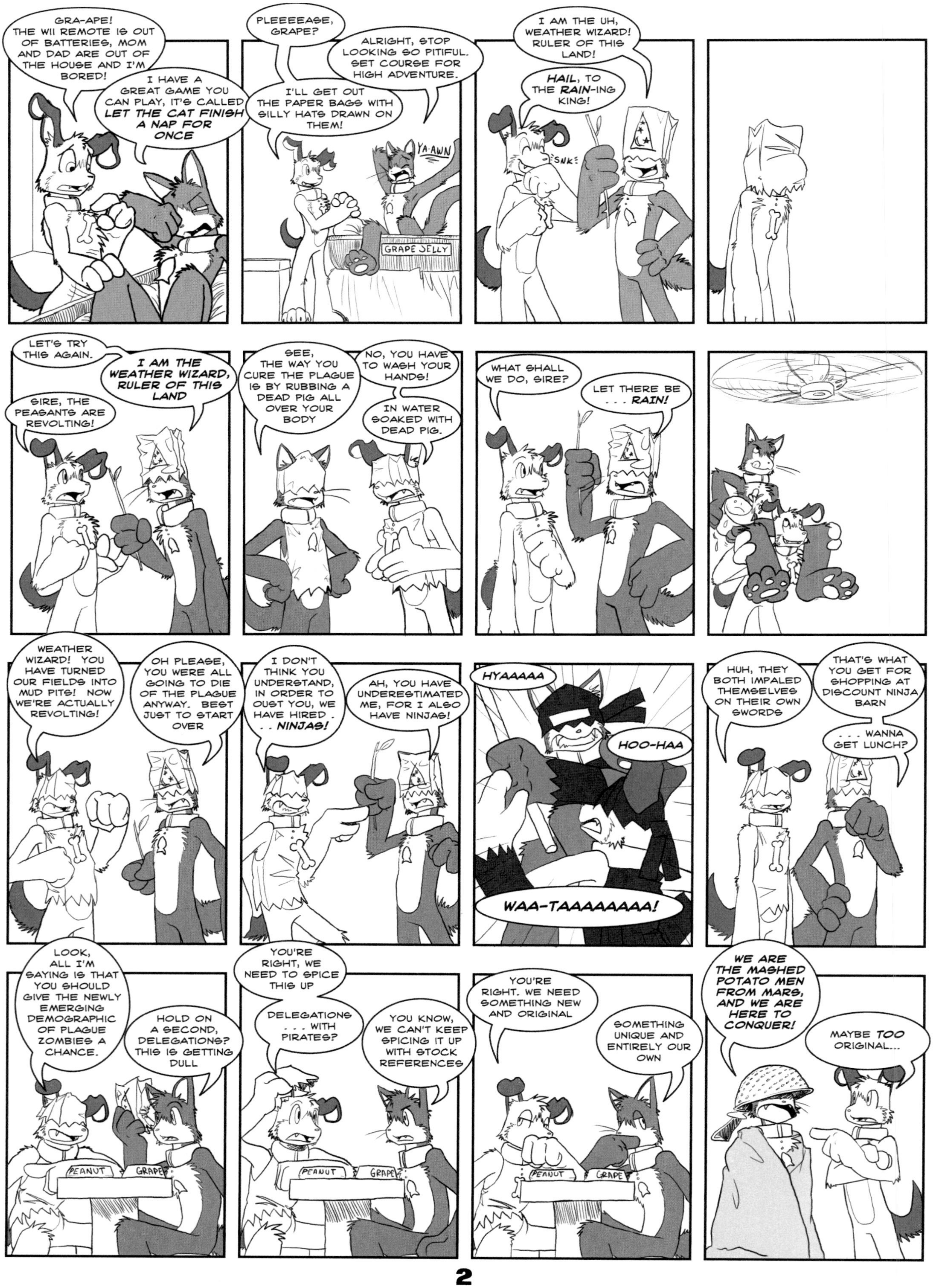

GRA-APE! THE WII REMOTE IS OUT OF BATTERIES, MOM AND DAD ARE OUT OF THE HOUSE AND I'M BORED!
I HAVE A GREAT GAME YOU CAN PLAY, IT'S CALLED LET THE CAT FINISH A NAP FOR ONCE
PLEEEEASE, GRAPE?
ALRIGHT, STOP LOOKING SO PITIFUL. SET COURSE FOR HIGH ADVENTURE.
I'LL GET OUT THE PAPER BAGS WITH SILLY HATS DRAWN ON THEM!
YA-AWN
GRAPE JELLY
I AM THE UH, WEATHER WIZARD! RULER OF THIS LAND!
HAIL, TO THE RAIN-ING KING!
SNK
LET'S TRY THIS AGAIN.
I AM THE WEATHER WIZARD, RULER OF THIS LAND
SIRE, THE PEASANTS ARE REVOLTING!
SEE, THE WAY YOU CURE THE PLAGUE IS BY RUBBING A DEAD PIG ALL OVER YOUR BODY
NO, YOU HAVE TO WASH YOUR HANDS!
IN WATER SOAKED WITH DEAD PIG.
WHAT SHALL WE DO, SIRE?
LET THERE BE . . . RAIN!
WEATHER WIZARD! YOU HAVE TURNED OUR FIELDS INTO MUD PITS! NOW WE'RE ACTUALLY REVOLTING!
OH PLEASE, YOU WERE ALL GOING TO DIE OF THE PLAGUE ANYWAY. BEST JUST TO START OVER
I DON'T THINK YOU UNDERSTAND, IN ORDER TO OUST YOU, WE HAVE HIRED . . . NINJAS!
AH, YOU HAVE UNDERESTIMATED ME, FOR I ALSO HAVE NINJAS!
HYAAAAA
HOO-HAA
WAA-TAAAAAAAA!
HUH, THEY BOTH IMPALED THEMSELVES ON THEIR OWN SWORDS
THAT'S WHAT YOU GET FOR SHOPPING AT DISCOUNT NINJA BARN
. . . WANNA GET LUNCH?
LOOK, ALL I'M SAYING IS THAT YOU SHOULD GIVE THE NEWLY EMERGING DEMOGRAPHIC OF PLAGUE ZOMBIES A CHANCE.
HOLD ON A SECOND, DELEGATIONS? THIS IS GETTING DULL
PEANUT
GRAPE
YOU'RE RIGHT, WE NEED TO SPICE THIS UP
DELEGATIONS . . . WITH PIRATES?
YOU KNOW, WE CAN'T KEEP SPICING IT UP WITH STOCK REFERENCES
PEANUT
GRAPE
YOU'RE RIGHT. WE NEED SOMETHING NEW AND ORIGINAL
SOMETHING UNIQUE AND ENTIRELY OUR OWN
PEANUT
GRAPE
WE ARE THE MASHED POTATO MEN FROM MARS, AND WE ARE HERE TO CONQUER!
MAYBE TOO ORIGINAL...

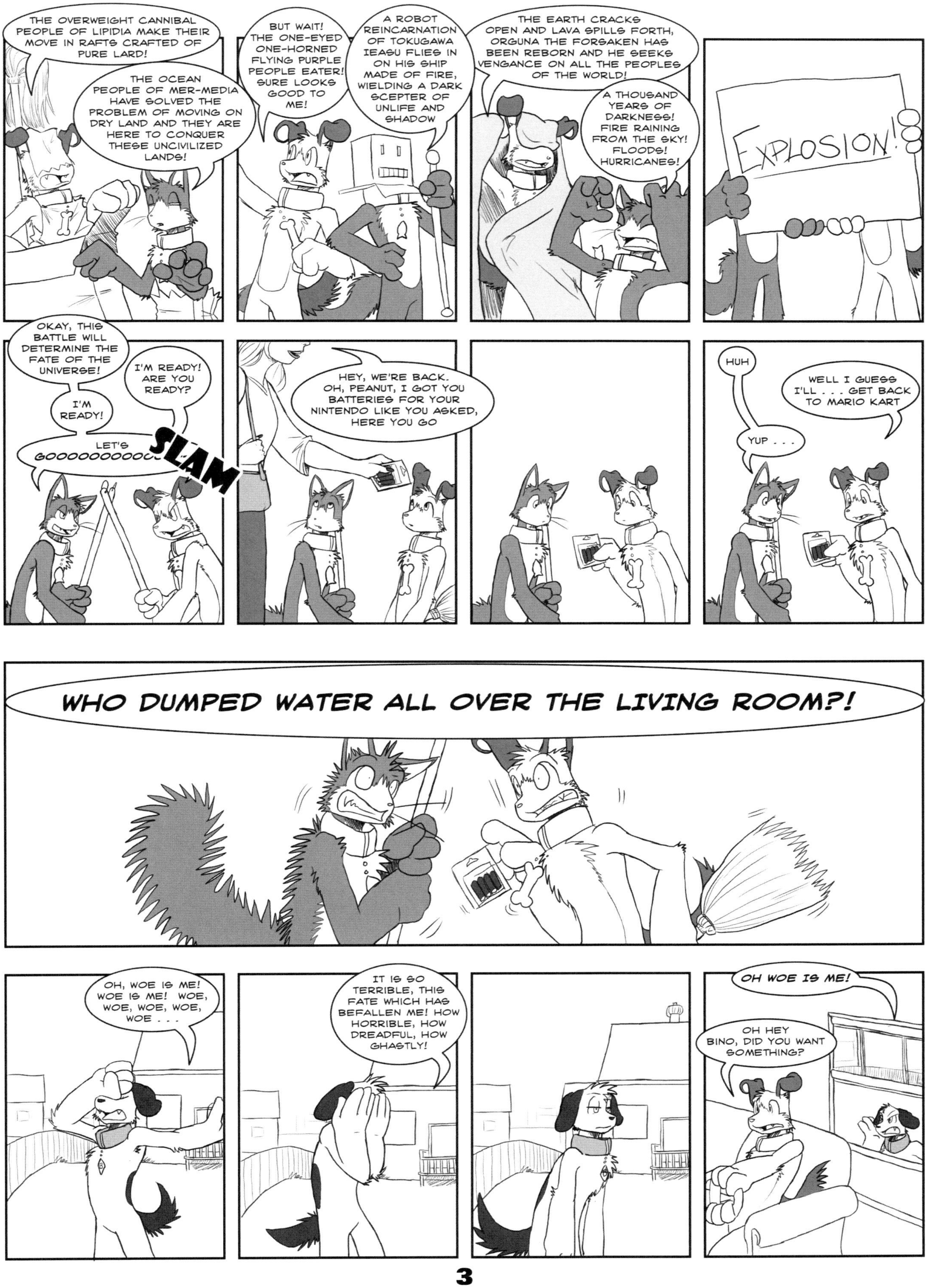
THE OVERWEIGHT CANNIBAL PEOPLE OF LIPIDIA MAKE THEIR MOVE IN RAFTS CRAFTED OF PURE LARD!
THE OCEAN PEOPLE OF MER-MEDIA HAVE SOLVED THE PROBLEM OF MOVING ON DRY LAND AND THEY ARE HERE TO CONQUER THESE UNCIVILIZED LANDS!
BUT WAIT! THE ONE-EYED ONE-HORNED FLYING PURPLE PEOPLE EATER! SURE LOOKS GOOD TO ME!
A ROBOT REINCARNATION OF TOKUGAWA IEASU FLIES IN ON HIS SHIP MADE OF FIRE, WIELDING A DARK SCEPTER OF UNLIFE AND SHADOW
THE EARTH CRACKS OPEN AND LAVA SPILLS FORTH, ORGUNA THE FORSAKEN HAS BEEN REBORN AND HE SEEKS VENGANCE ON ALL THE PEOPLES OF THE WORLD!
A THOUSAND YEARS OF DARKNESS! FIRE RAINING FROM THE SKY! FLOODS! HURRICANES!
EXPLOSION!
OKAY, THIS BATTLE WILL DETERMINE THE FATE OF THE UNIVERSE!
I'M READY! ARE YOU READY?
I'M READY!
LET'S GOOOOOOOOOOO
SLAM
HEY, WE'RE BACK. OH, PEANUT, I GOT YOU BATTERIES FOR YOUR NINTENDO LIKE YOU ASKED, HERE YOU GO
HUH
YUP . . .
WELL I GUESS I'LL . . . GET BACK TO MARIO KART
WHO DUMPED WATER ALL OVER THE LIVING ROOM?!
OH, WOE IS ME! WOE IS ME! WOE, WOE, WOE, WOE, WOE . . .
IT IS SO TERRIBLE, THIS FATE WHICH HAS BEFALLEN ME! HOW HORRIBLE, HOW DREADFUL, HOW GHASTLY!
OH WOE IS ME!
OH HEY BINO, DID YOU WANT SOMETHING?

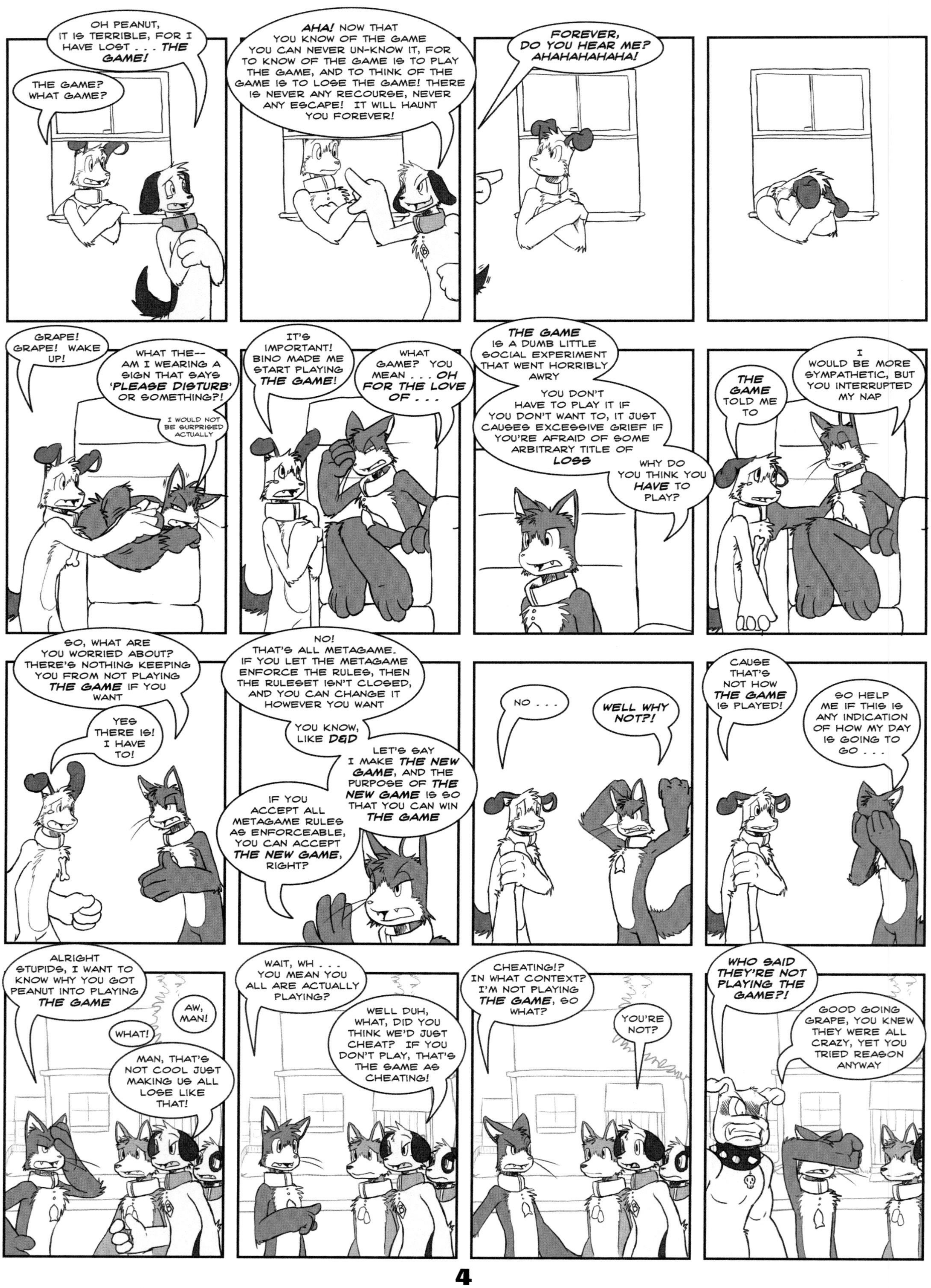

OH PEANUT, IT IS TERRIBLE, FOR I HAVE LOST . . . THE GAME!
THE GAME? WHAT GAME?
AHA! NOW THAT YOU KNOW OF THE GAME YOU CAN NEVER UN-KNOW IT, FOR TO KNOW OF THE GAME IS TO PLAY THE GAME, AND TO THINK OF THE GAME IS TO LOSE THE GAME! THERE IS NEVER ANY RECOURSE, NEVER ANY ESCAPE! IT WILL HAUNT YOU FOREVER!
FOREVER, DO YOU HEAR ME? AHAHAHAHAHA!
GRAPE! GRAPE! WAKE UP!
WHAT THE-- AM I WEARING A SIGN THAT SAYS 'PLEASE DISTURB' OR SOMETHING?!
I WOULD NOT BE SURPRISED ACTUALLY
IT'S IMPORTANT! BINO MADE ME START PLAYING THE GAME!
WHAT GAME? YOU MEAN . . . OH FOR THE LOVE OF . . .
THE GAME IS A DUMB LITTLE SOCIAL EXPERIMENT THAT WENT HORRIBLY AWRY
YOU DON'T HAVE TO PLAY IT IF YOU DON'T WANT TO, IT JUST CAUSES EXCESSIVE GRIEF IF YOU'RE AFRAID OF SOME ARBITRARY TITLE OF LOSS
WHY DO YOU THINK YOU HAVE TO PLAY?
THE GAME TOLD ME TO
I WOULD BE MORE SYMPATHETIC, BUT YOU INTERRUPTED MY NAP
SO, WHAT ARE YOU WORRIED ABOUT? THERE'S NOTHING KEEPING YOU FROM NOT PLAYING THE GAME IF YOU WANT
YES THERE IS! I HAVE TO!
NO! THAT'S ALL METAGAME. IF YOU LET THE METAGAME ENFORCE THE RULES, THEN THE RULESET ISN'T CLOSED, AND YOU CAN CHANGE IT HOWEVER YOU WANT
YOU KNOW, LIKE D&D
LET'S SAY I MAKE THE NEW GAME, AND THE PURPOSE OF THE NEW GAME IS SO THAT YOU CAN WIN THE GAME
IF YOU ACCEPT ALL METAGAME RULES AS ENFORCEABLE, YOU CAN ACCEPT THE NEW GAME, RIGHT?
NO . . .
WELL WHY NOT?!
CAUSE THAT'S NOT HOW THE GAME IS PLAYED!
SO HELP ME IF THIS IS ANY INDICATION OF HOW MY DAY IS GOING TO GO . . .
ALRIGHT STUPIDS, I WANT TO KNOW WHY YOU GOT PEANUT INTO PLAYING THE GAME
AW, MAN!
WHAT!
MAN, THAT'S NOT COOL JUST MAKING US ALL LOSE LIKE THAT!
WAIT, WH . . . YOU MEAN YOU ALL ARE ACTUALLY PLAYING?
WELL DUH, WHAT, DID YOU THINK WE'D JUST CHEAT? IF YOU DON'T PLAY, THAT'S THE SAME AS CHEATING!
CHEATING!? IN WHAT CONTEXT? I'M NOT PLAYING THE GAME, SO WHAT?
YOU'RE NOT?
WHO SAID THEY'RE NOT PLAYING THE GAME?!
GOOD GOING GRAPE, YOU KNEW THEY WERE ALL CRAZY, YET YOU TRIED REASON ANYWAY

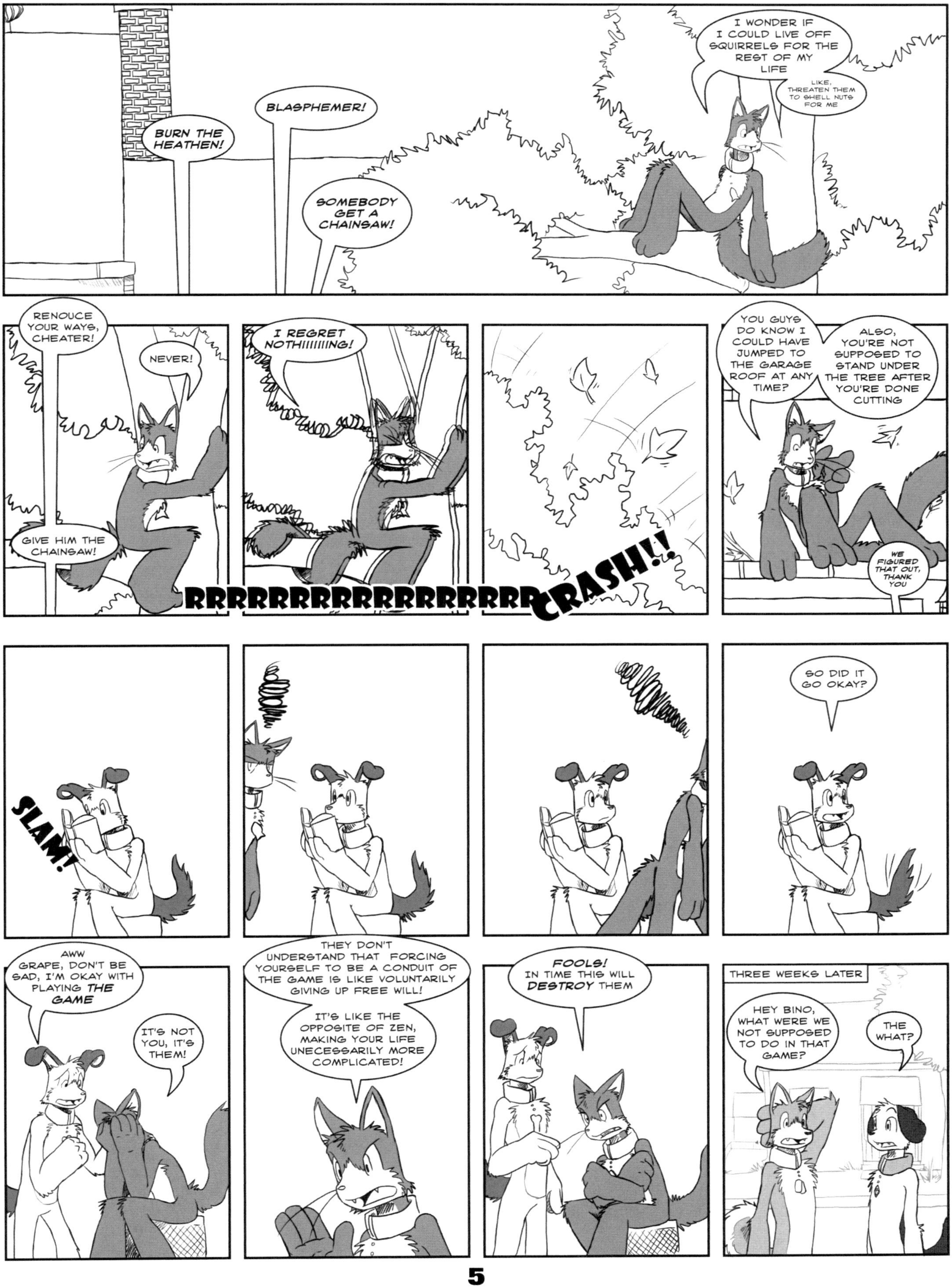
BURN THE HEATHEN!
BLASPHEMER!
SOMEBODY GET A CHAINSAW!
I WONDER IF I COULD LIVE OFF SQUIRRELS FOR THE REST OF MY LIFE
LIKE, THREATEN THEM TO SHELL NUTS FOR ME
RENOUCE YOUR WAYS, CHEATER!
NEVER!
GIVE HIM THE CHAINSAW!
I REGRET NOTHIIIIIIING!
RRRRRRRRRRRRRRRRRRR
CRASH!!
YOU GUYS DO KNOW I COULD HAVE JUMPED TO THE GARAGE ROOF AT ANY TIME?
ALSO, YOU'RE NOT SUPPOSED TO STAND UNDER THE TREE AFTER YOU'RE DONE CUTTING
WE FIGURED THAT OUT, THANK YOU
SLAM!
SO DID IT GO OKAY?
AWW GRAPE, DON'T BE SAD, I'M OKAY WITH PLAYING THE GAME
IT'S NOT YOU, IT'S THEM!
THEY DON'T UNDERSTAND THAT FORCING YOURSELF TO BE A CONDUIT OF THE GAME IS LIKE VOLUNTARILY GIVING UP FREE WILL!
IT'S LIKE THE OPPOSITE OF ZEN, MAKING YOUR LIFE UNECESSARILY MORE COMPLICATED!
FOOLS! IN TIME THIS WILL DESTROY THEM
THREE WEEKS LATER
HEY BINO, WHAT WERE WE NOT SUPPOSED TO DO IN THAT GAME?
THE WHAT?

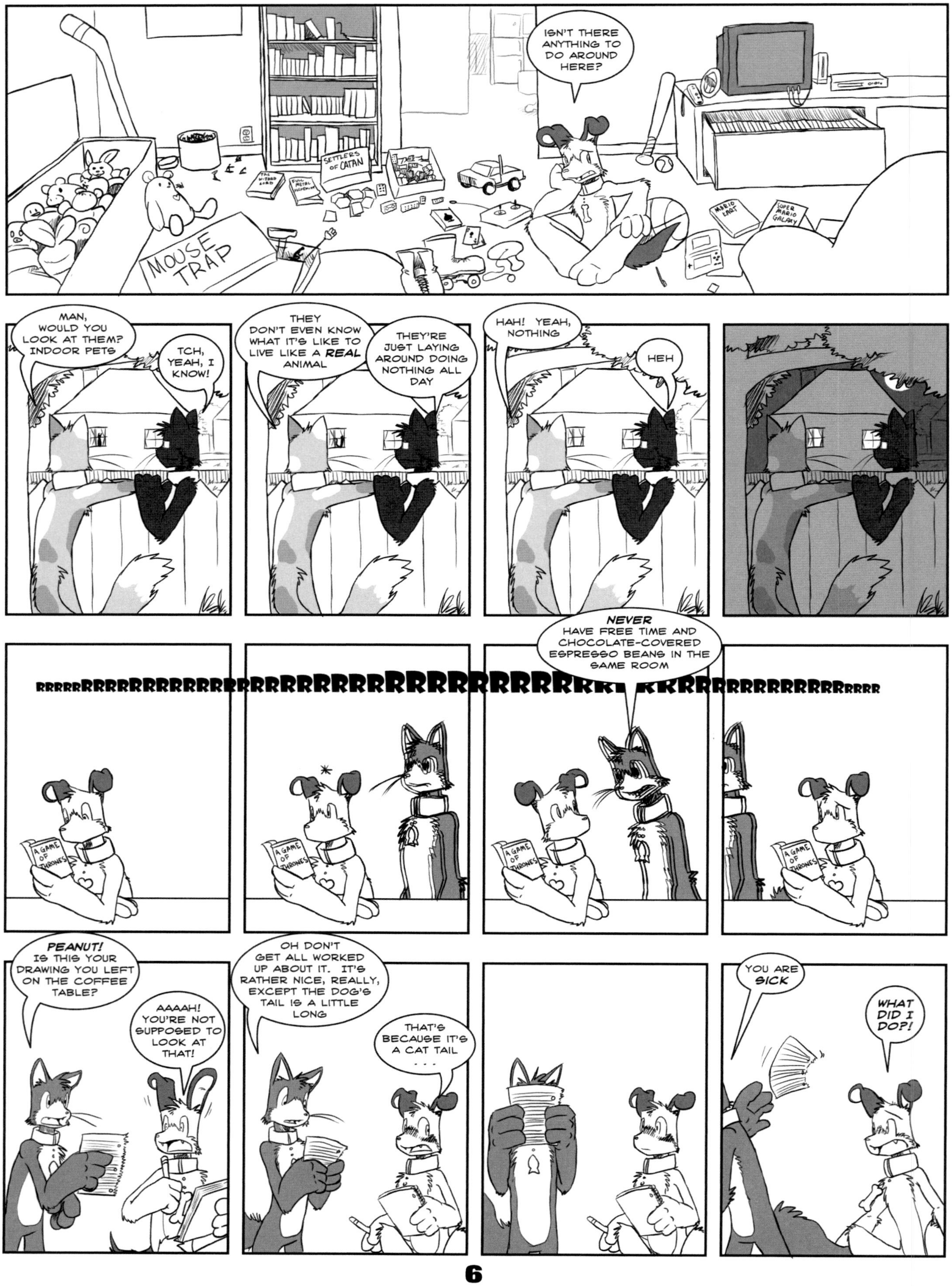
ISN'T THERE ANYTHING TO DO AROUND HERE?
MOUSE TRAP
SETTLERS OF CATAN
MAN, WOULD YOU LOOK AT THEM? INDOOR PETS
TCH, YEAH, I KNOW!
THEY DON'T EVEN KNOW WHAT IT'S LIKE TO LIVE LIKE A **REAL** ANIMAL
THEY'RE JUST LAYING AROUND DOING NOTHING ALL DAY
HAH! YEAH, NOTHING
HEH
RRRRRRRRRRRRRRRRRRRRRRRRRRRRRRRRRRRRRRRRRRRRRRRRRRRRRRRRRRRRRRRRR
A GAME OF THRONES
NEVER HAVE FREE TIME AND CHOCOLATE-COVERED ESPRESSO BEANS IN THE SAME ROOM
PEANUT! IS THIS YOUR DRAWING YOU LEFT ON THE COFFEE TABLE?
AAAAH! YOU'RE NOT SUPPOSED TO LOOK AT THAT!
OH DON'T GET ALL WORKED UP ABOUT IT. IT'S RATHER NICE, REALLY, EXCEPT THE DOG'S TAIL IS A LITTLE LONG
THAT'S BECAUSE IT'S A CAT TAIL . . .
YOU ARE **SICK**
WHAT DID I DO?!

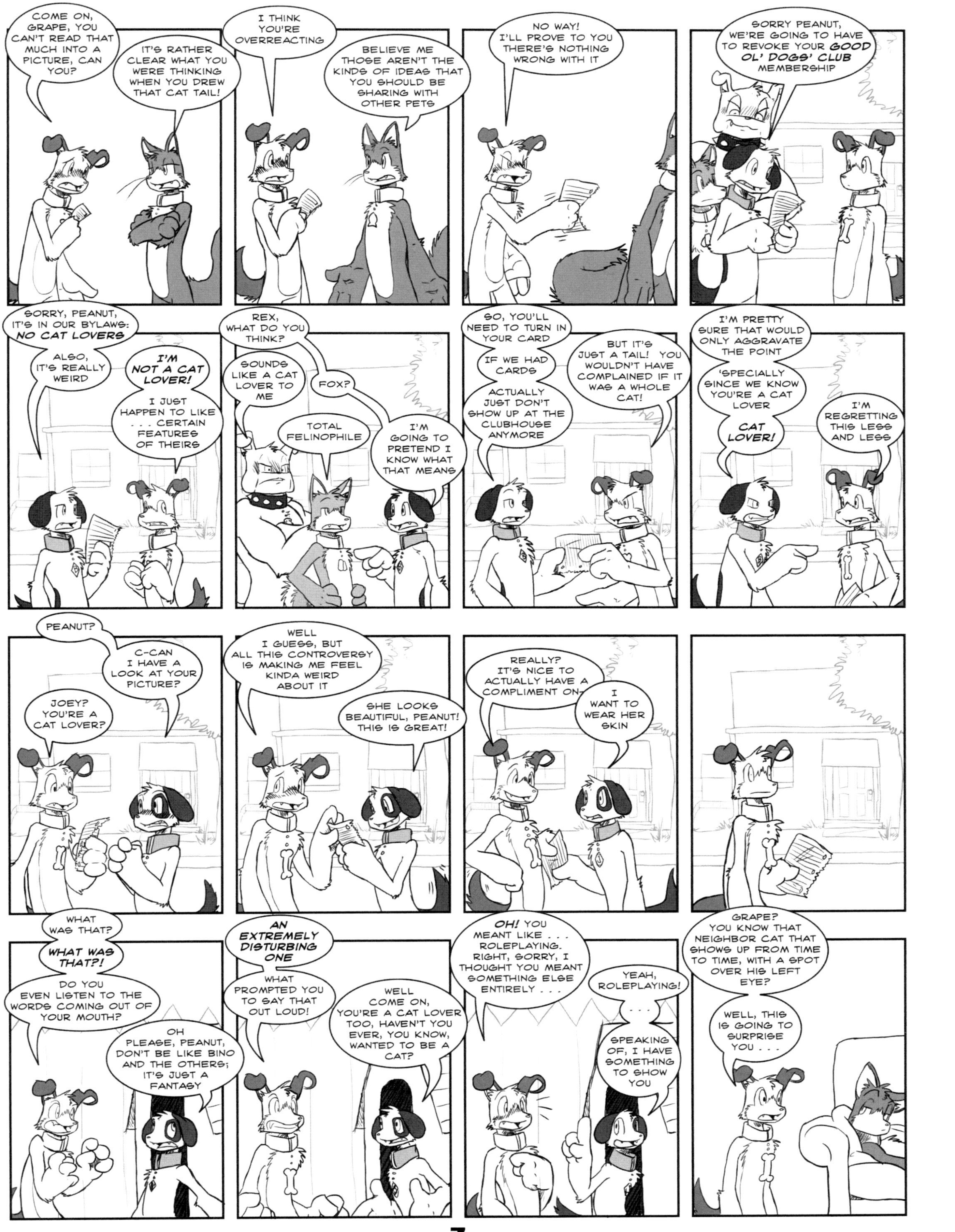

COME ON, GRAPE, YOU CAN'T READ THAT MUCH INTO A PICTURE, CAN YOU?
IT'S RATHER CLEAR WHAT YOU WERE THINKING WHEN YOU DREW THAT CAT TAIL!
I THINK YOU'RE OVERREACTING
BELIEVE ME THOSE AREN'T THE KINDS OF IDEAS THAT YOU SHOULD BE SHARING WITH OTHER PETS
NO WAY! I'LL PROVE TO YOU THERE'S NOTHING WRONG WITH IT
SORRY PEANUT, WE'RE GOING TO HAVE TO REVOKE YOUR GOOD OL' DOGS' CLUB MEMBERSHIP
SORRY, PEANUT, IT'S IN OUR BYLAWS: NO CAT LOVERS
ALSO, IT'S REALLY WEIRD
I'M NOT A CAT LOVER!
I JUST HAPPEN TO LIKE . . . CERTAIN FEATURES OF THEIRS
REX, WHAT DO YOU THINK?
SOUNDS LIKE A CAT LOVER TO ME
FOX?
TOTAL FELINOPHILE
I'M GOING TO PRETEND I KNOW WHAT THAT MEANS
SO, YOU'LL NEED TO TURN IN YOUR CARD
IF WE HAD CARDS
ACTUALLY JUST DON'T SHOW UP AT THE CLUBHOUSE ANYMORE
BUT IT'S JUST A TAIL! YOU WOULDN'T HAVE COMPLAINED IF IT WAS A WHOLE CAT!
I'M PRETTY SURE THAT WOULD ONLY AGGRAVATE THE POINT
'SPECIALLY SINCE WE KNOW YOU'RE A CAT LOVER
CAT LOVER!
I'M REGRETTING THIS LESS AND LESS
PEANUT?
C-CAN I HAVE A LOOK AT YOUR PICTURE?
JOEY? YOU'RE A CAT LOVER?
WELL I GUESS, BUT ALL THIS CONTROVERSY IS MAKING ME FEEL KINDA WEIRD ABOUT IT
SHE LOOKS BEAUTIFUL, PEANUT! THIS IS GREAT!
REALLY? IT'S NICE TO ACTUALLY HAVE A COMPLIMENT ON–
I WANT TO WEAR HER SKIN
WHAT WAS THAT?
WHAT WAS THAT?!
DO YOU EVEN LISTEN TO THE WORDS COMING OUT OF YOUR MOUTH?
OH PLEASE, PEANUT, DON'T BE LIKE BINO AND THE OTHERS; IT'S JUST A FANTASY
AN EXTREMELY DISTURBING ONE
WHAT PROMPTED YOU TO SAY THAT OUT LOUD!
WELL COME ON, YOU'RE A CAT LOVER TOO, HAVEN'T YOU EVER, YOU KNOW, WANTED TO BE A CAT?
OH! YOU MEANT LIKE . . . ROLEPLAYING. RIGHT, SORRY, I THOUGHT YOU MEANT SOMETHING ELSE ENTIRELY . . .
YEAH, ROLEPLAYING!
. . .
SPEAKING OF, I HAVE SOMETHING TO SHOW YOU
GRAPE? YOU KNOW THAT NEIGHBOR CAT THAT SHOWS UP FROM TIME TO TIME, WITH A SPOT OVER HIS LEFT EYE?
WELL, THIS IS GOING TO SURPRISE YOU . . .

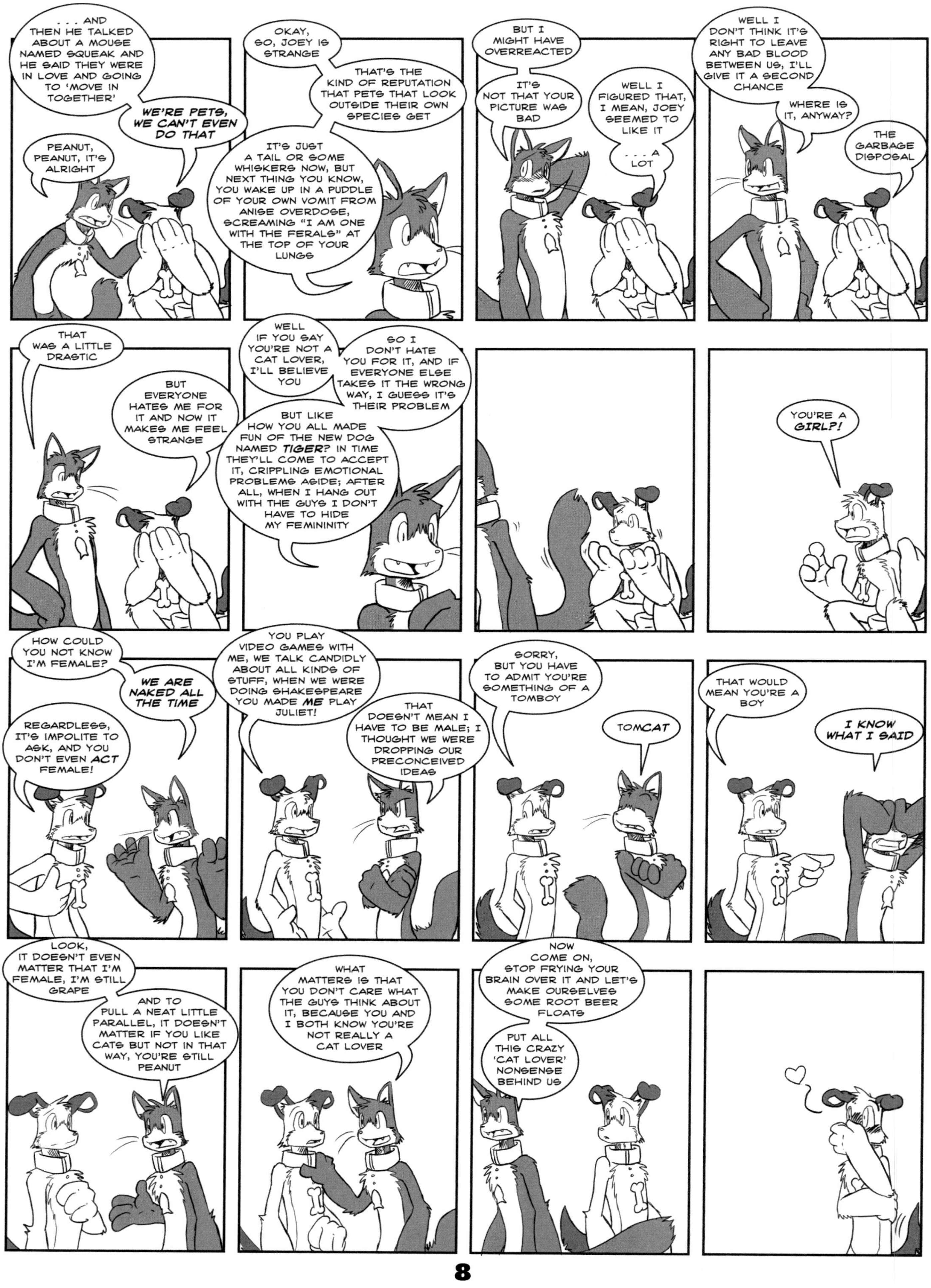
. . . AND THEN HE TALKED ABOUT A MOUSE NAMED SQUEAK AND HE SAID THEY WERE IN LOVE AND GOING TO 'MOVE IN TOGETHER'
WE'RE PETS, WE CAN'T EVEN DO THAT
PEANUT, PEANUT, IT'S ALRIGHT
OKAY, SO, JOEY IS STRANGE
THAT'S THE KIND OF REPUTATION THAT PETS THAT LOOK OUTSIDE THEIR OWN SPECIES GET
IT'S JUST A TAIL OR SOME WHISKERS NOW, BUT NEXT THING YOU KNOW, YOU WAKE UP IN A PUDDLE OF YOUR OWN VOMIT FROM ANISE OVERDOSE, SCREAMING "I AM ONE WITH THE FERALS" AT THE TOP OF YOUR LUNGS
BUT I MIGHT HAVE OVERREACTED
IT'S NOT THAT YOUR PICTURE WAS BAD
WELL I FIGURED THAT, I MEAN, JOEY SEEMED TO LIKE IT
. . . A LOT
WELL I DON'T THINK IT'S RIGHT TO LEAVE ANY BAD BLOOD BETWEEN US, I'LL GIVE IT A SECOND CHANCE
WHERE IS IT, ANYWAY?
THE GARBAGE DISPOSAL
THAT WAS A LITTLE DRASTIC
BUT EVERYONE HATES ME FOR IT AND NOW IT MAKES ME FEEL STRANGE
WELL IF YOU SAY YOU'RE NOT A CAT LOVER, I'LL BELIEVE YOU
SO I DON'T HATE YOU FOR IT, AND IF EVERYONE ELSE TAKES IT THE WRONG WAY, I GUESS IT'S THEIR PROBLEM
BUT LIKE HOW YOU ALL MADE FUN OF THE NEW DOG NAMED TIGER? IN TIME THEY'LL COME TO ACCEPT IT, CRIPPLING EMOTIONAL PROBLEMS ASIDE; AFTER ALL, WHEN I HANG OUT WITH THE GUYS I DON'T HAVE TO HIDE MY FEMININITY
YOU'RE A GIRL?!
HOW COULD YOU NOT KNOW I'M FEMALE?
WE ARE NAKED ALL THE TIME
REGARDLESS, IT'S IMPOLITE TO ASK, AND YOU DON'T EVEN ACT FEMALE!
YOU PLAY VIDEO GAMES WITH ME, WE TALK CANDIDLY ABOUT ALL KINDS OF STUFF, WHEN WE WERE DOING SHAKESPEARE YOU MADE ME PLAY JULIET!
THAT DOESN'T MEAN I HAVE TO BE MALE; I THOUGHT WE WERE DROPPING OUR PRECONCEIVED IDEAS
SORRY, BUT YOU HAVE TO ADMIT YOU'RE SOMETHING OF A TOMBOY
TOMCAT
THAT WOULD MEAN YOU'RE A BOY
I KNOW WHAT I SAID
LOOK, IT DOESN'T EVEN MATTER THAT I'M FEMALE, I'M STILL GRAPE
AND TO PULL A NEAT LITTLE PARALLEL, IT DOESN'T MATTER IF YOU LIKE CATS BUT NOT IN THAT WAY, YOU'RE STILL PEANUT
WHAT MATTERS IS THAT YOU DON'T CARE WHAT THE GUYS THINK ABOUT IT, BECAUSE YOU AND I BOTH KNOW YOU'RE NOT REALLY A CAT LOVER
NOW COME ON, STOP FRYING YOUR BRAIN OVER IT AND LET'S MAKE OURSELVES SOME ROOT BEER FLOATS
PUT ALL THIS CRAZY 'CAT LOVER' NONSENSE BEHIND US

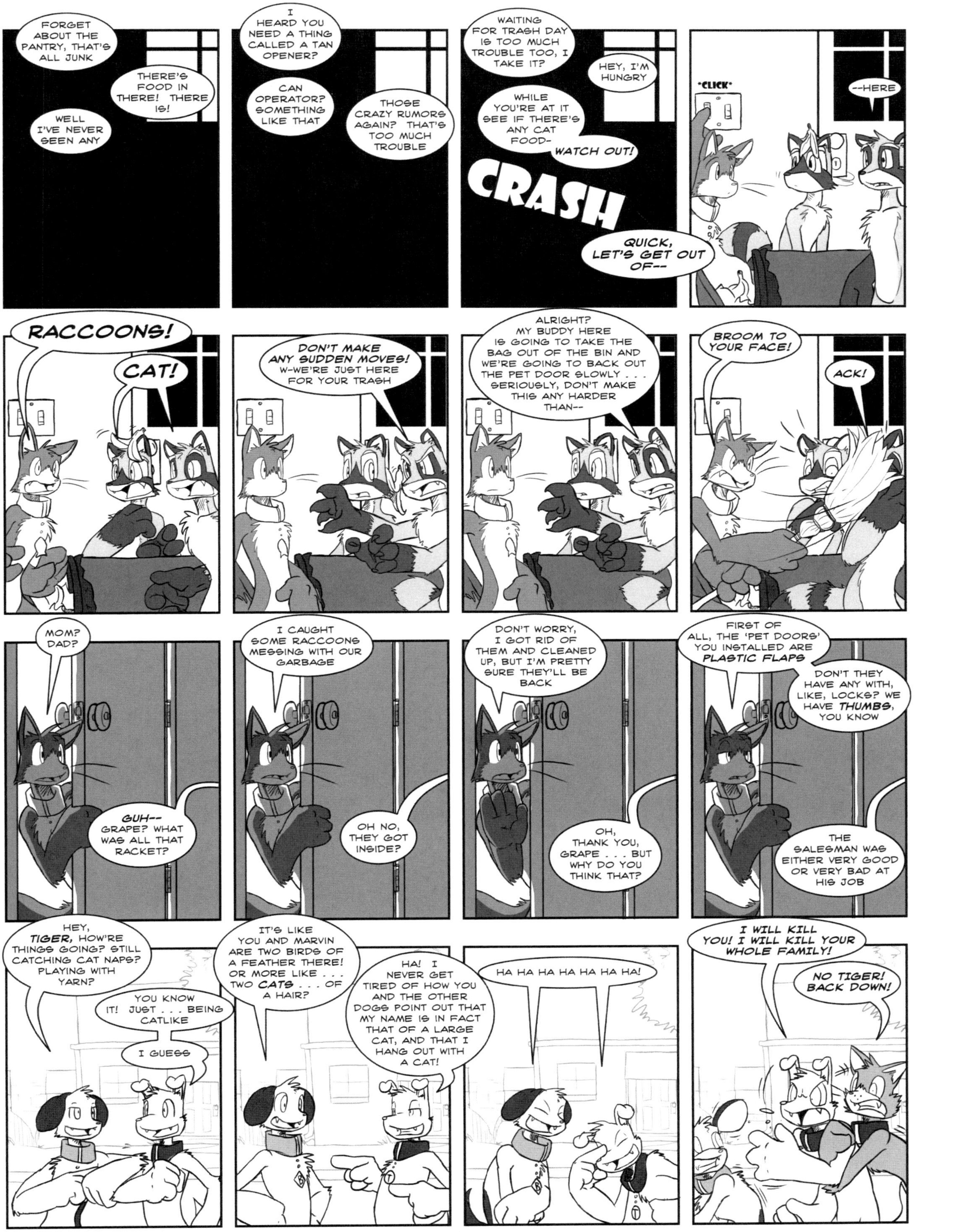

FORGET ABOUT THE PANTRY, THAT'S ALL JUNK
THERE'S FOOD IN THERE! THERE IS!
WELL I'VE NEVER SEEN ANY
I HEARD YOU NEED A THING CALLED A TAN OPENER?
CAN OPERATOR? SOMETHING LIKE THAT
THOSE CRAZY RUMORS AGAIN? THAT'S TOO MUCH TROUBLE
WAITING FOR TRASH DAY IS TOO MUCH TROUBLE TOO, I TAKE IT?
HEY, I'M HUNGRY
WHILE YOU'RE AT IT SEE IF THERE'S ANY CAT FOOD-
WATCH OUT!
CRASH
QUICK, LET'S GET OUT OF--
CLICK
--HERE
RACCOONS!
CAT!
DON'T MAKE ANY SUDDEN MOVES! W-WE'RE JUST HERE FOR YOUR TRASH
ALRIGHT? MY BUDDY HERE IS GOING TO TAKE THE BAG OUT OF THE BIN AND WE'RE GOING TO BACK OUT THE PET DOOR SLOWLY . . . SERIOUSLY, DON'T MAKE THIS ANY HARDER THAN--
BROOM TO YOUR FACE!
ACK!
MOM? DAD?
GUH-- GRAPE? WHAT WAS ALL THAT RACKET?
I CAUGHT SOME RACCOONS MESSING WITH OUR GARBAGE
OH NO, THEY GOT INSIDE?
DON'T WORRY, I GOT RID OF THEM AND CLEANED UP, BUT I'M PRETTY SURE THEY'LL BE BACK
OH, THANK YOU, GRAPE . . . BUT WHY DO YOU THINK THAT?
FIRST OF ALL, THE 'PET DOORS' YOU INSTALLED ARE PLASTIC FLAPS
DON'T THEY HAVE ANY WITH, LIKE, LOCKS? WE HAVE THUMBS, YOU KNOW
THE SALESMAN WAS EITHER VERY GOOD OR VERY BAD AT HIS JOB
HEY, TIGER, HOW'RE THINGS GOING? STILL CATCHING CAT NAPS? PLAYING WITH YARN?
YOU KNOW IT! JUST . . . BEING CATLIKE
I GUESS
IT'S LIKE YOU AND MARVIN ARE TWO BIRDS OF A FEATHER THERE! OR MORE LIKE . . . TWO CATS . . . OF A HAIR?
HA! I NEVER GET TIRED OF HOW YOU AND THE OTHER DOGS POINT OUT THAT MY NAME IS IN FACT THAT OF A LARGE CAT, AND THAT I HANG OUT WITH A CAT!
HA HA HA HA HA HA HA!
I WILL KILL YOU! I WILL KILL YOUR WHOLE FAMILY!
NO TIGER! BACK DOWN!

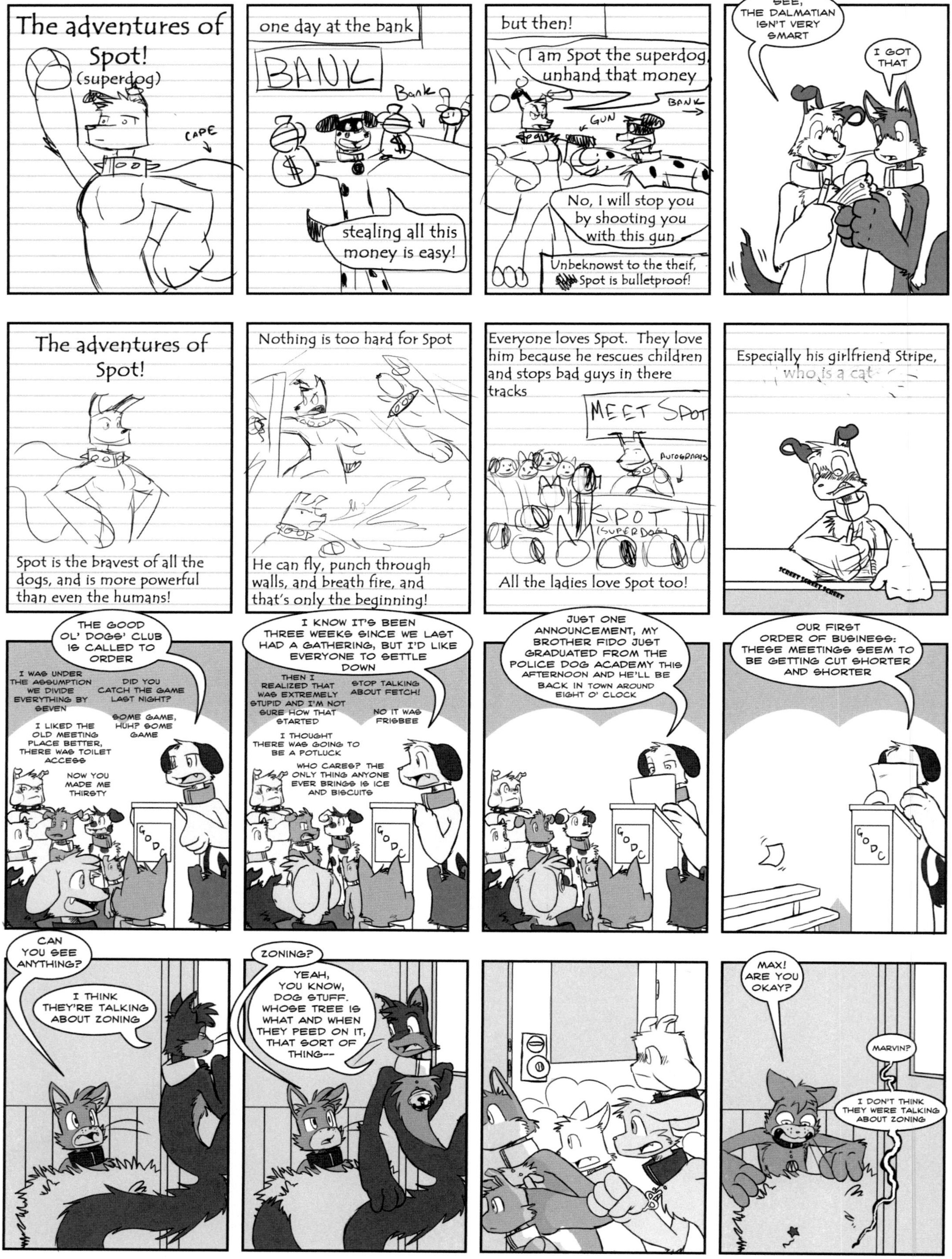
The adventures of Spot! (superdog)
CAPE
one day at the bank
BANK
Bank
stealing all this money is easy!
but then!
I am Spot the superdog, unhand that money
BANK
GUN
No, I will stop you by shooting you with this gun
Unbeknowst to the theif, Spot is bulletproof!
SEE, THE DALMATIAN ISN'T VERY SMART
I GOT THAT
The adventures of Spot!
Spot is the bravest of all the dogs, and is more powerful than even the humans!
Nothing is too hard for Spot
He can fly, punch through walls, and breath fire, and that's only the beginning!
Everyone loves Spot. They love him because he rescues children and stops bad guys in there tracks
MEET SPOT
SPOT (SUPERDOG)
All the ladies love Spot too!
Especially his girlfriend Stripe, who is a cat
SCREET SCREET SCREET
THE GOOD OL' DOGS' CLUB IS CALLED TO ORDER
I WAS UNDER THE ASSUMPTION WE DIVIDE EVERYTHING BY SEVEN
DID YOU CATCH THE GAME LAST NIGHT?
I LIKED THE OLD MEETING PLACE BETTER, THERE WAS TOILET ACCESS
SOME GAME, HUH? SOME GAME
NOW YOU MADE ME THIRSTY
GODC
I KNOW IT'S BEEN THREE WEEKS SINCE WE LAST HAD A GATHERING, BUT I'D LIKE EVERYONE TO SETTLE DOWN
THEN I REALIZED THAT WAS EXTREMELY STUPID AND I'M NOT SURE HOW THAT STARTED
STOP TALKING ABOUT FETCH!
NO IT WAS FRISBEE
I THOUGHT THERE WAS GOING TO BE A POTLUCK
WHO CARES? THE ONLY THING ANYONE EVER BRINGS IS ICE AND BISCUITS
GODC
JUST ONE ANNOUNCEMENT, MY BROTHER FIDO JUST GRADUATED FROM THE POLICE DOG ACADEMY THIS AFTERNOON AND HE'LL BE BACK IN TOWN AROUND EIGHT O' CLOCK
GODC
OUR FIRST ORDER OF BUSINESS: THESE MEETINGS SEEM TO BE GETTING CUT SHORTER AND SHORTER
GODC
CAN YOU SEE ANYTHING?
I THINK THEY'RE TALKING ABOUT ZONING
ZONING?
YEAH, YOU KNOW, DOG STUFF. WHOSE TREE IS WHAT AND WHEN THEY PEED ON IT, THAT SORT OF THING--
MAX! ARE YOU OKAY?
MARVIN?
I DON'T THINK THEY WERE TALKING ABOUT ZONING

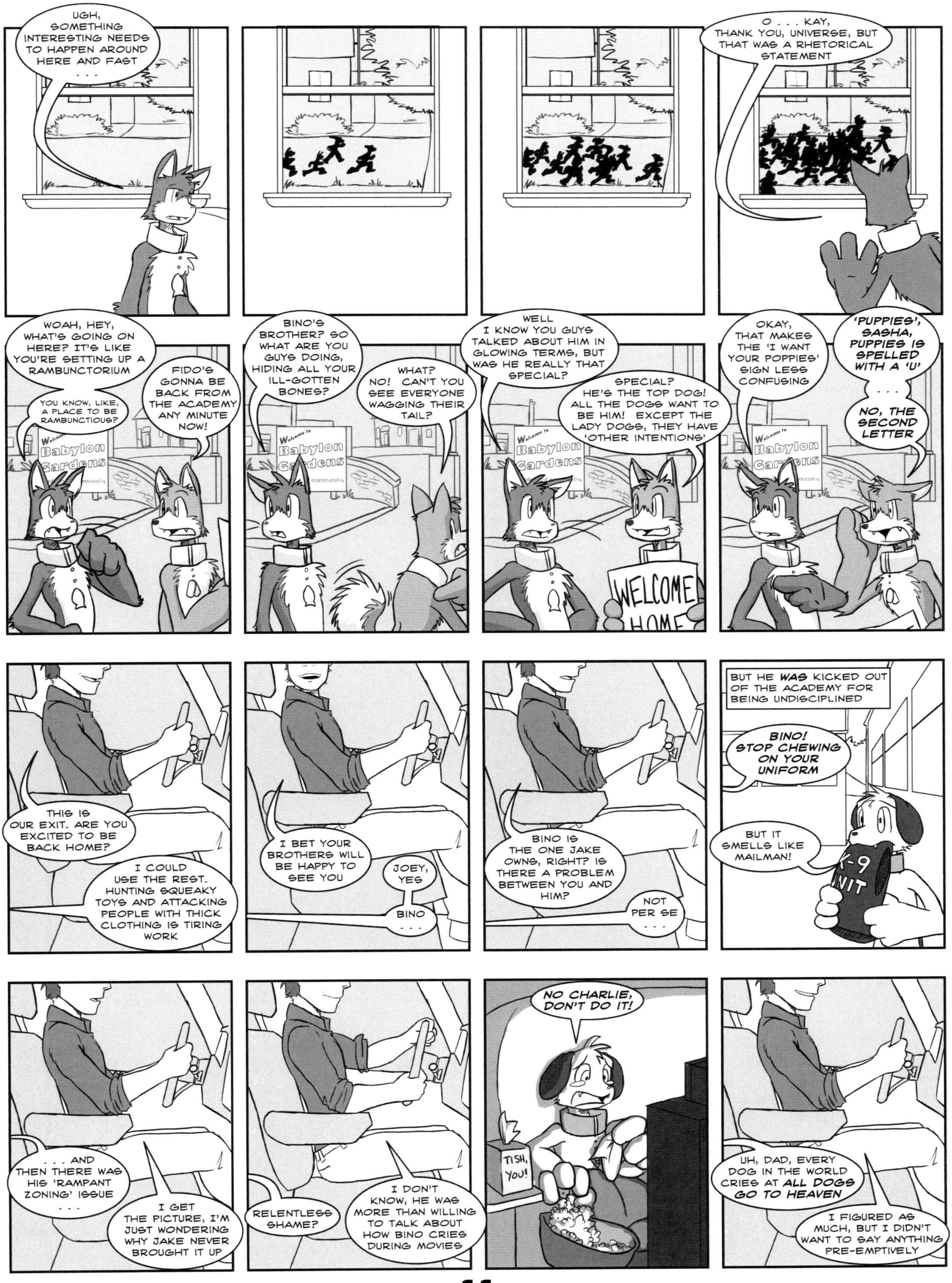

UGH, SOMETHING INTERESTING NEEDS TO HAPPEN AROUND HERE AND FAST . . .
O . . . KAY, THANK YOU, UNIVERSE, BUT THAT WAS A RHETORICAL STATEMENT
WOAH, HEY, WHAT'S GOING ON HERE? IT'S LIKE YOU'RE SETTING UP A RAMBUNCTORIUM
YOU KNOW, LIKE, A PLACE TO BE RAMBUNCTIOUS?
FIDO'S GONNA BE BACK FROM THE ACADEMY ANY MINUTE NOW!
Welcome to Babylon Gardens community
BINO'S BROTHER? SO WHAT ARE YOU GUYS DOING, HIDING ALL YOUR ILL-GOTTEN BONES?
WHAT? NO! CAN'T YOU SEE EVERYONE WAGGING THEIR TAIL?
WELL I KNOW YOU GUYS TALKED ABOUT HIM IN GLOWING TERMS, BUT WAS HE REALLY THAT SPECIAL?
SPECIAL? HE'S THE TOP DOG! ALL THE DOGS WANT TO BE HIM! EXCEPT THE LADY DOGS, THEY HAVE 'OTHER INTENTIONS'
WELCOME HOME
OKAY, THAT MAKES THE 'I WANT YOUR POPPIES' SIGN LESS CONFUSING
'PUPPIES', SASHA, PUPPIES IS SPELLED WITH A 'U'
. . .
NO, THE SECOND LETTER
THIS IS OUR EXIT. ARE YOU EXCITED TO BE BACK HOME?
I COULD USE THE REST. HUNTING SQUEAKY TOYS AND ATTACKING PEOPLE WITH THICK CLOTHING IS TIRING WORK
I BET YOUR BROTHERS WILL BE HAPPY TO SEE YOU
JOEY, YES
BINO . . .
BINO IS THE ONE JAKE OWNS, RIGHT? IS THERE A PROBLEM BETWEEN YOU AND HIM?
NOT PER SE . . .
BUT HE WAS KICKED OUT OF THE ACADEMY FOR BEING UNDISCIPLINED
BINO! STOP CHEWING ON YOUR UNIFORM
BUT IT SMELLS LIKE MAILMAN!
K-9 UNIT
. . . AND THEN THERE WAS HIS 'RAMPANT ZONING' ISSUE . . .
I GET THE PICTURE, I'M JUST WONDERING WHY JAKE NEVER BROUGHT IT UP
RELENTLESS SHAME?
I DON'T KNOW, HE WAS MORE THAN WILLING TO TALK ABOUT HOW BINO CRIES DURING MOVIES
NO CHARLIE, DON'T DO IT!
TISH, YOU!
UH, DAD, EVERY DOG IN THE WORLD CRIES AT ALL DOGS GO TO HEAVEN
I FIGURED AS MUCH, BUT I DIDN'T WANT TO SAY ANYTHING PRE-EMPTIVELY

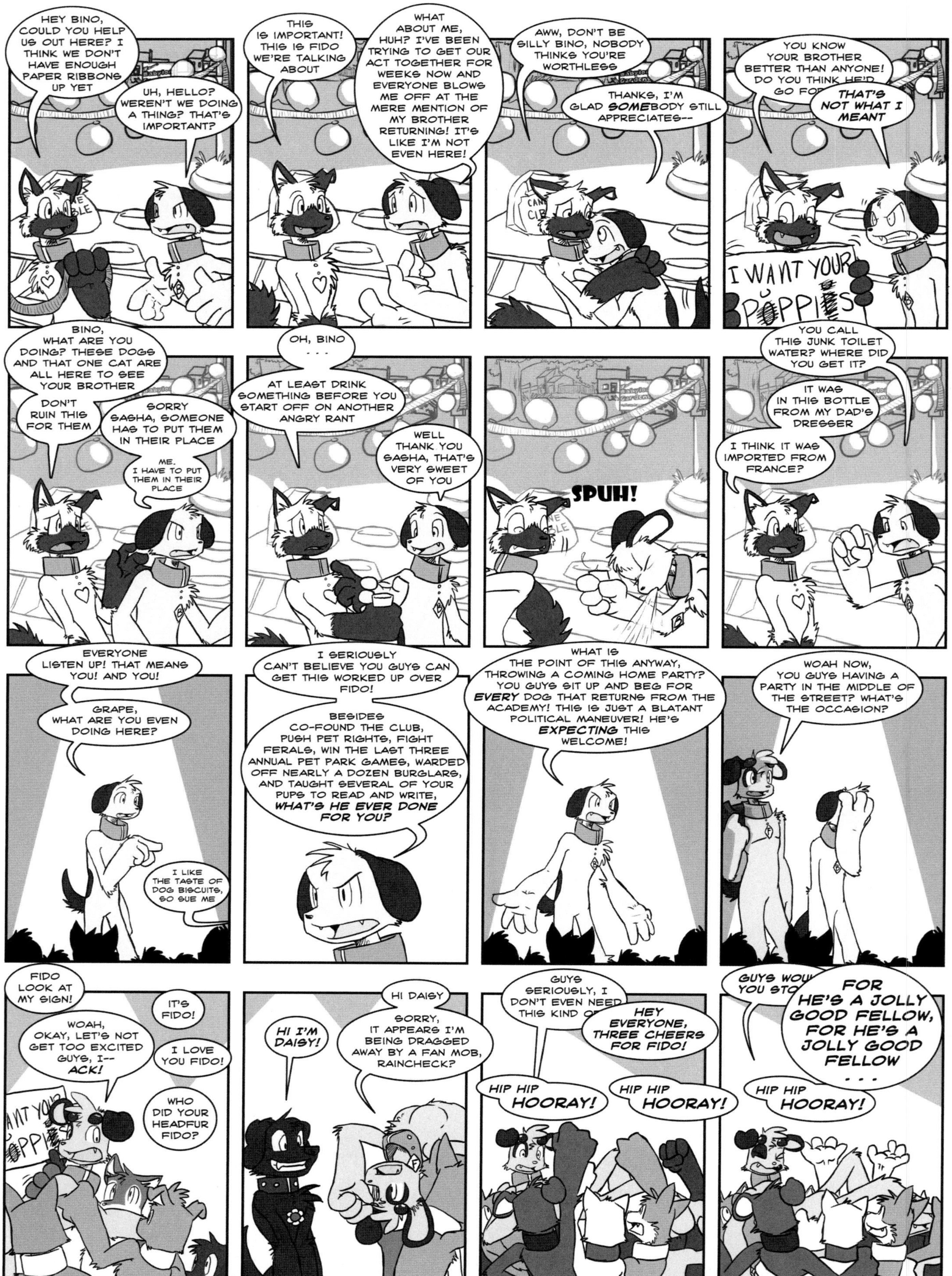

HEY BINO, COULD YOU HELP US OUT HERE? I THINK WE DON'T HAVE ENOUGH PAPER RIBBONS UP YET
UH, HELLO? WEREN'T WE DOING A THING? THAT'S IMPORTANT?
THIS IS IMPORTANT! THIS IS FIDO WE'RE TALKING ABOUT
WHAT ABOUT ME, HUH? I'VE BEEN TRYING TO GET OUR ACT TOGETHER FOR WEEKS NOW AND EVERYONE BLOWS ME OFF AT THE MERE MENTION OF MY BROTHER RETURNING! IT'S LIKE I'M NOT EVEN HERE!
AWW, DON'T BE SILLY BINO, NOBODY THINKS YOU'RE WORTHLESS
THANKS, I'M GLAD **SOME**BODY STILL APPRECIATES--
YOU KNOW YOUR BROTHER BETTER THAN ANYONE! DO YOU THINK HE'D GO FO
THAT'S NOT WHAT I MEANT
I WANT YOUR PUPPIES
BINO, WHAT ARE YOU DOING? THESE DOGS AND THAT ONE CAT ARE ALL HERE TO SEE YOUR BROTHER
DON'T RUIN THIS FOR THEM
SORRY SASHA, SOMEONE HAS TO PUT THEM IN THEIR PLACE
ME. I HAVE TO PUT THEM IN THEIR PLACE
OH, BINO . . .
AT LEAST DRINK SOMETHING BEFORE YOU START OFF ON ANOTHER ANGRY RANT
WELL THANK YOU SASHA, THAT'S VERY SWEET OF YOU
SPUH!
YOU CALL THIS JUNK TOILET WATER? WHERE DID YOU GET IT?
IT WAS IN THIS BOTTLE FROM MY DAD'S DRESSER
I THINK IT WAS IMPORTED FROM FRANCE?
EVERYONE LISTEN UP! THAT MEANS YOU! AND YOU!
GRAPE, WHAT ARE YOU EVEN DOING HERE?
I LIKE THE TASTE OF DOG BISCUITS, SO SUE ME
I SERIOUSLY CAN'T BELIEVE YOU GUYS CAN GET THIS WORKED UP OVER FIDO!
BESIDES CO-FOUND THE CLUB, PUSH PET RIGHTS, FIGHT FERALS, WIN THE LAST THREE ANNUAL PET PARK GAMES, WARDED OFF NEARLY A DOZEN BURGLARS, AND TAUGHT SEVERAL OF YOUR PUPS TO READ AND WRITE, ***WHAT'S HE EVER DONE FOR YOU?***
WHAT IS THE POINT OF THIS ANYWAY, THROWING A COMING HOME PARTY? YOU GUYS SIT UP AND BEG FOR ***EVERY*** DOG THAT RETURNS FROM THE ACADEMY! THIS IS JUST A BLATANT POLITICAL MANEUVER! HE'S ***EXPECTING*** THIS WELCOME!
WOAH NOW, YOU GUYS HAVING A PARTY IN THE MIDDLE OF THE STREET? WHAT'S THE OCCASION?
FIDO LOOK AT MY SIGN!
IT'S FIDO!
WOAH, OKAY, LET'S NOT GET TOO EXCITED GUYS, I-- ***ACK!***
I LOVE YOU FIDO!
WHO DID YOUR HEADFUR FIDO?
HI DAISY
HI I'M DAISY!
SORRY, IT APPEARS I'M BEING DRAGGED AWAY BY A FAN MOB, RAINCHECK?
GUYS SERIOUSLY, I DON'T EVEN NEED THIS KIND O
HEY EVERYONE, THREE CHEERS FOR FIDO!
HIP HIP **HOORAY!**
HIP HIP **HOORAY!**
GUYS WOU YOU STO
FOR HE'S A JOLLY GOOD FELLOW, FOR HE'S A JOLLY GOOD FELLOW . . .
HIP HIP **HOORAY!**

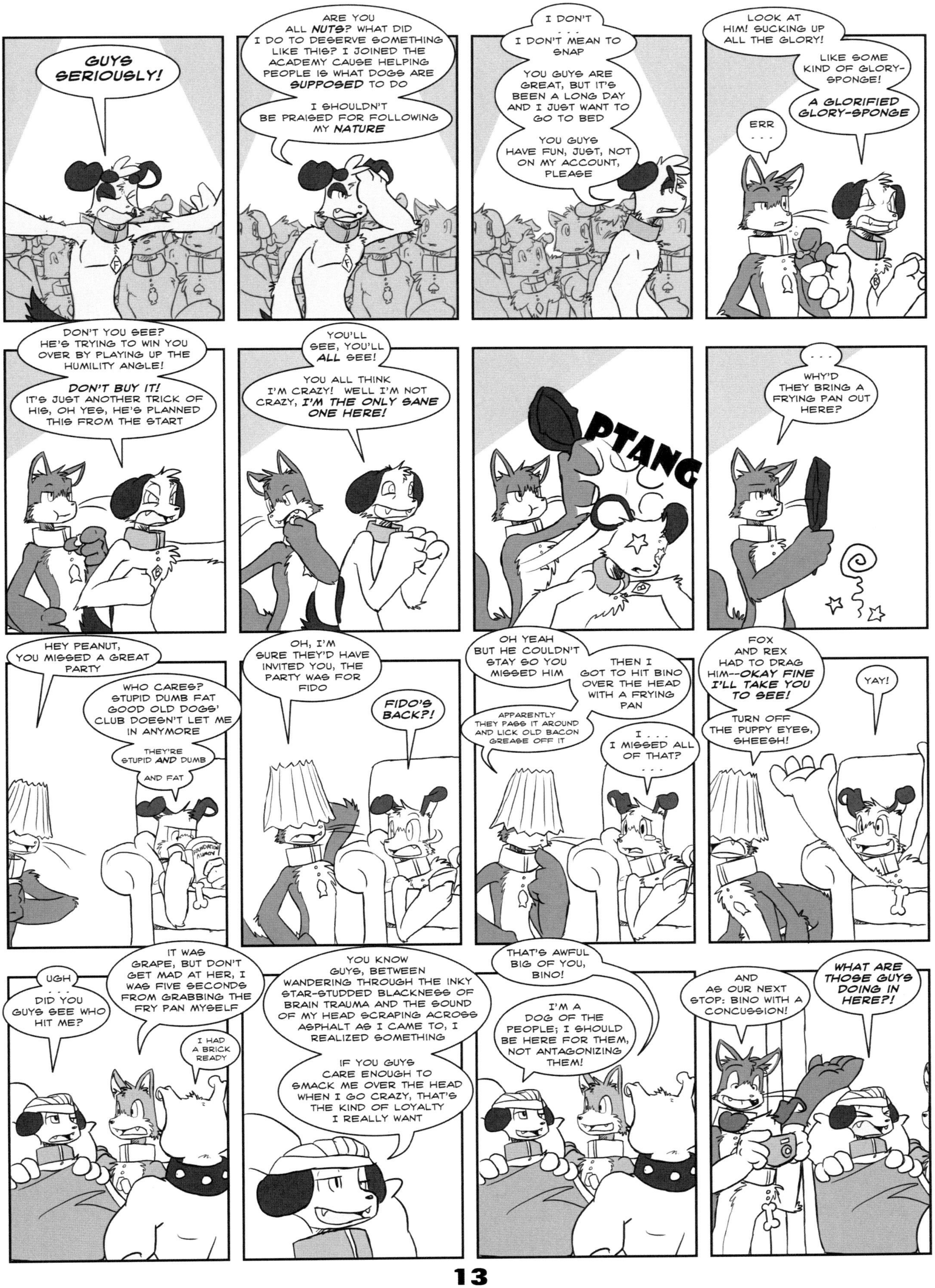
GUYS SERIOUSLY!
ARE YOU ALL NUTS? WHAT DID I DO TO DESERVE SOMETHING LIKE THIS? I JOINED THE ACADEMY CAUSE HELPING PEOPLE IS WHAT DOGS ARE SUPPOSED TO DO
I SHOULDN'T BE PRAISED FOR FOLLOWING MY NATURE
I DON'T . . . I DON'T MEAN TO SNAP
YOU GUYS ARE GREAT, BUT IT'S BEEN A LONG DAY AND I JUST WANT TO GO TO BED
YOU GUYS HAVE FUN, JUST, NOT ON MY ACCOUNT, PLEASE
LOOK AT HIM! SUCKING UP ALL THE GLORY!
LIKE SOME KIND OF GLORY-SPONGE!
A GLORIFIED GLORY-SPONGE
ERR . . .
DON'T YOU SEE? HE'S TRYING TO WIN YOU OVER BY PLAYING UP THE HUMILITY ANGLE!
DON'T BUY IT! IT'S JUST ANOTHER TRICK OF HIS, OH YES, HE'S PLANNED THIS FROM THE START
YOU'LL SEE, YOU'LL ALL SEE!
YOU ALL THINK I'M CRAZY! WELL I'M NOT CRAZY, I'M THE ONLY SANE ONE HERE!
PTANG
. . .
WHY'D THEY BRING A FRYING PAN OUT HERE?
HEY PEANUT, YOU MISSED A GREAT PARTY
WHO CARES? STUPID DUMB FAT GOOD OLD DOGS' CLUB DOESN'T LET ME IN ANYMORE
THEY'RE STUPID AND DUMB
AND FAT
FOUNDATION ASIMOV
OH, I'M SURE THEY'D HAVE INVITED YOU, THE PARTY WAS FOR FIDO
FIDO'S BACK?!
OH YEAH BUT HE COULDN'T STAY SO YOU MISSED HIM
THEN I GOT TO HIT BINO OVER THE HEAD WITH A FRYING PAN
APPARENTLY THEY PASS IT AROUND AND LICK OLD BACON GREASE OFF IT
I . . . I MISSED ALL OF THAT? . . .
FOX AND REX HAD TO DRAG HIM--OKAY FINE I'LL TAKE YOU TO SEE!
TURN OFF THE PUPPY EYES, SHEESH!
YAY!
UGH . . . DID YOU GUYS SEE WHO HIT ME?
IT WAS GRAPE, BUT DON'T GET MAD AT HER, I WAS FIVE SECONDS FROM GRABBING THE FRY PAN MYSELF
I HAD A BRICK READY
YOU KNOW GUYS, BETWEEN WANDERING THROUGH THE INKY STAR-STUDDED BLACKNESS OF BRAIN TRAUMA AND THE SOUND OF MY HEAD SCRAPING ACROSS ASPHALT AS I CAME TO, I REALIZED SOMETHING
IF YOU GUYS CARE ENOUGH TO SMACK ME OVER THE HEAD WHEN I GO CRAZY, THAT'S THE KIND OF LOYALTY I REALLY WANT
THAT'S AWFUL BIG OF YOU, BINO!
I'M A DOG OF THE PEOPLE; I SHOULD BE HERE FOR THEM, NOT ANTAGONIZING THEM!
AND AS OUR NEXT STOP: BINO WITH A CONCUSSION!
WHAT ARE THOSE GUYS DOING IN HERE?!

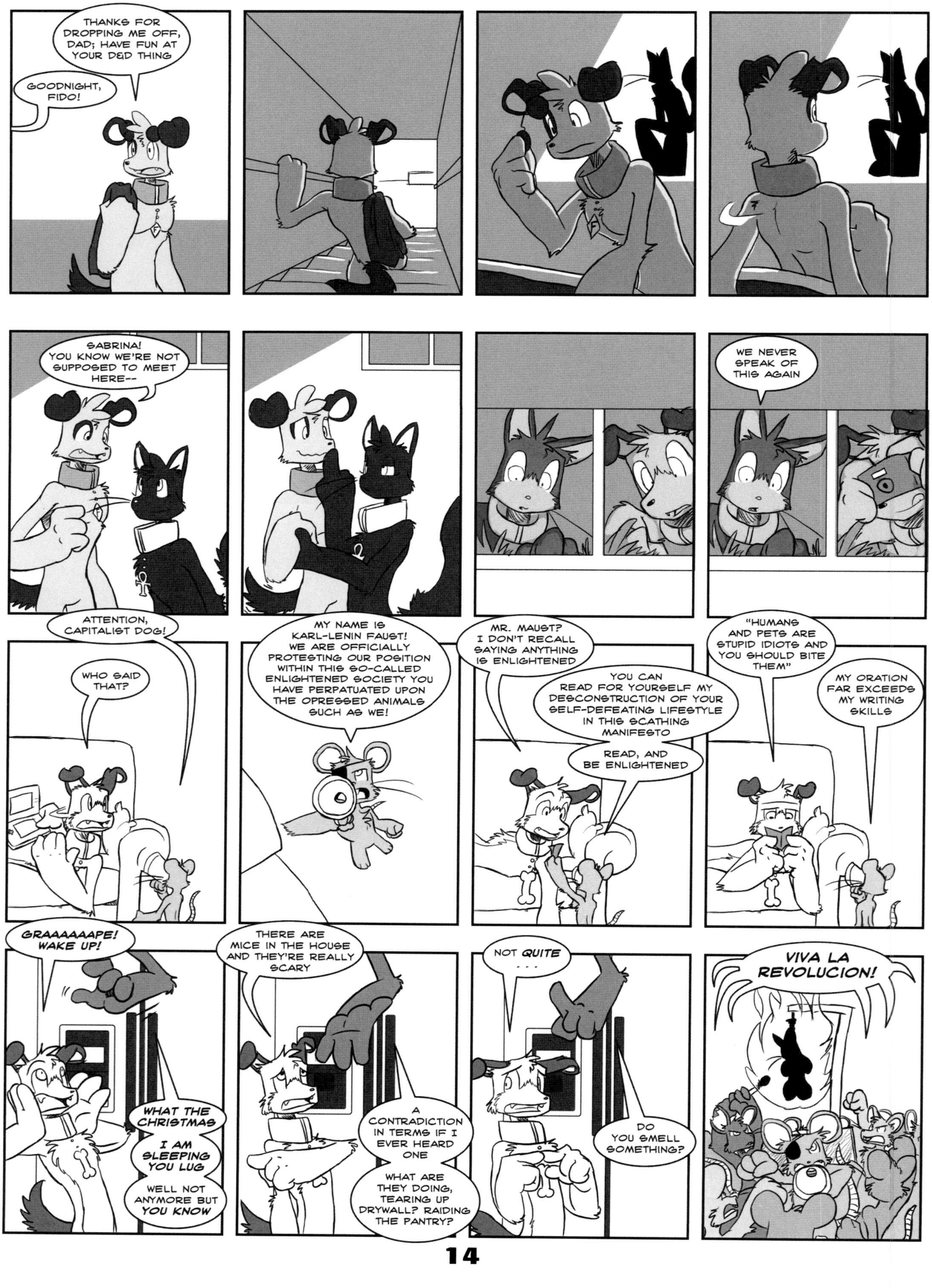

THANKS FOR DROPPING ME OFF, DAD; HAVE FUN AT YOUR D&D THING
GOODNIGHT, FIDO!
SABRINA! YOU KNOW WE'RE NOT SUPPOSED TO MEET HERE--
WE NEVER SPEAK OF THIS AGAIN
ATTENTION, CAPITALIST DOG!
WHO SAID THAT?
MY NAME IS KARL-LENIN FAUST! WE ARE OFFICIALLY PROTESTING OUR POSITION WITHIN THIS SO-CALLED ENLIGHTENED SOCIETY YOU HAVE PERPATUATED UPON THE OPRESSED ANIMALS SUCH AS WE!
MR. MAUST? I DON'T RECALL SAYING ANYTHING IS ENLIGHTENED
YOU CAN READ FOR YOURSELF MY DESCONSTRUCTION OF YOUR SELF-DEFEATING LIFESTYLE IN THIS SCATHING MANIFESTO
READ, AND BE ENLIGHTENED
"HUMANS AND PETS ARE STUPID IDIOTS AND YOU SHOULD BITE THEM"
MY ORATION FAR EXCEEDS MY WRITING SKILLS
GRAAAAAAPE! WAKE UP!
WHAT THE CHRISTMAS
I AM SLEEPING YOU LUG
WELL NOT ANYMORE BUT YOU KNOW
THERE ARE MICE IN THE HOUSE AND THEY'RE REALLY SCARY
A CONTRADICTION IN TERMS IF I EVER HEARD ONE
WHAT ARE THEY DOING, TEARING UP DRYWALL? RAIDING THE PANTRY?
NOT QUITE . . .
DO YOU SMELL SOMETHING?
VIVA LA REVOLUCION!

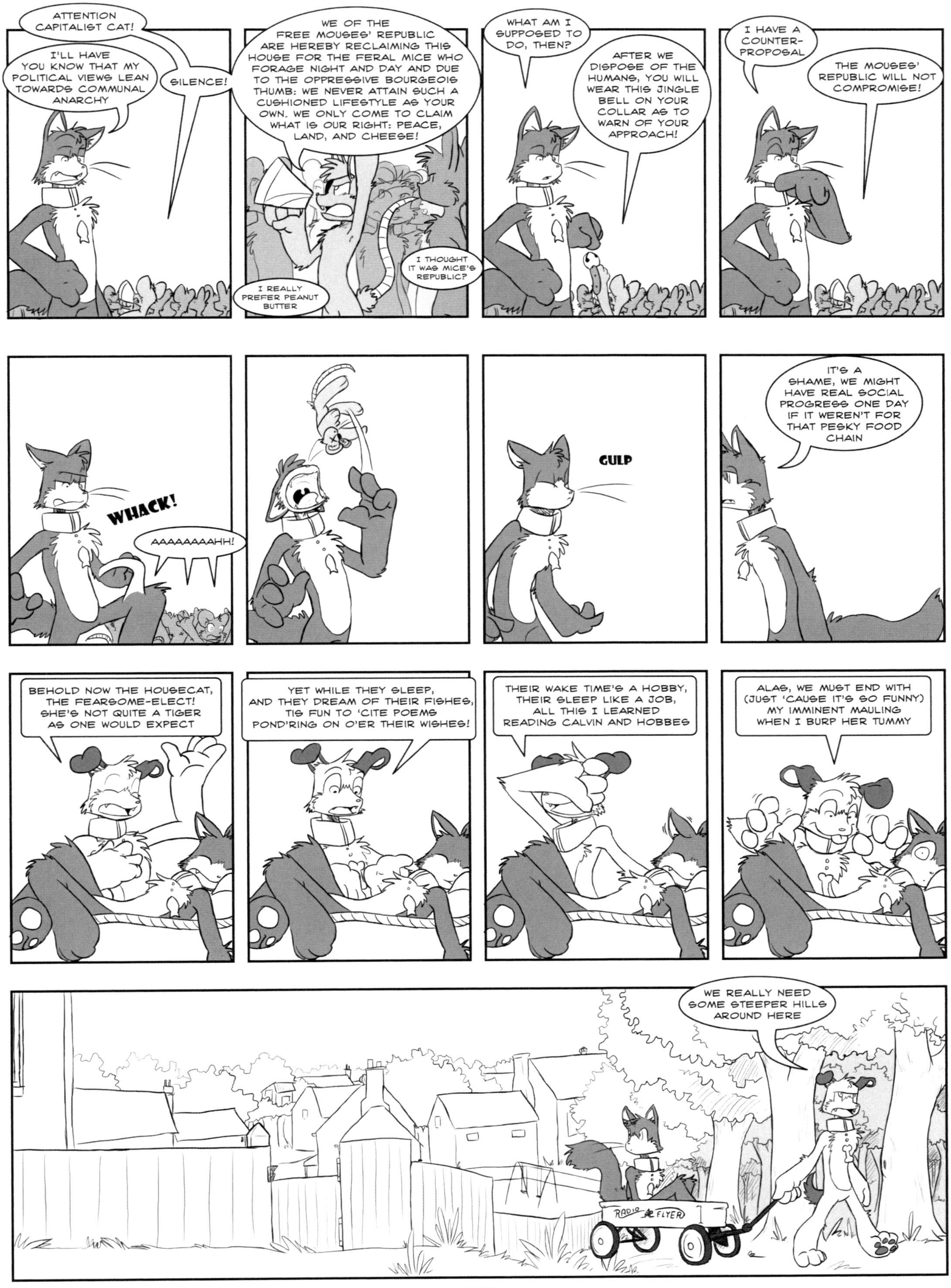

ATTENTION CAPITALIST CAT!
I'LL HAVE YOU KNOW THAT MY POLITICAL VIEWS LEAN TOWARDS COMMUNAL ANARCHY
SILENCE!
WE OF THE FREE MOUSES' REPUBLIC ARE HEREBY RECLAIMING THIS HOUSE FOR THE FERAL MICE WHO FORAGE NIGHT AND DAY AND DUE TO THE OPPRESSIVE BOURGEOIS THUMB: WE NEVER ATTAIN SUCH A CUSHIONED LIFESTYLE AS YOUR OWN. WE ONLY COME TO CLAIM WHAT IS OUR RIGHT: PEACE, LAND, AND CHEESE!
I REALLY PREFER PEANUT BUTTER
I THOUGHT IT WAS MICE'S REPUBLIC?
WHAT AM I SUPPOSED TO DO, THEN?
AFTER WE DISPOSE OF THE HUMANS, YOU WILL WEAR THIS JINGLE BELL ON YOUR COLLAR AS TO WARN OF YOUR APPROACH!
I HAVE A COUNTER-PROPOSAL
THE MOUSES' REPUBLIC WILL NOT COMPROMISE!
WHACK!
AAAAAAAAHH!
GULP
IT'S A SHAME, WE MIGHT HAVE REAL SOCIAL PROGRESS ONE DAY IF IT WEREN'T FOR THAT PESKY FOOD CHAIN
BEHOLD NOW THE HOUSECAT, THE FEARSOME-ELECT! SHE'S NOT QUITE A TIGER AS ONE WOULD EXPECT
YET WHILE THEY SLEEP, AND THEY DREAM OF THEIR FISHES, TIS FUN TO 'CITE POEMS POND'RING ON O'ER THEIR WISHES!
THEIR WAKE TIME'S A HOBBY, THEIR SLEEP LIKE A JOB, ALL THIS I LEARNED READING CALVIN AND HOBBES
ALAS, WE MUST END WITH (JUST 'CAUSE IT'S SO FUNNY) MY IMMINENT MAULING WHEN I BURP HER TUMMY
WE REALLY NEED SOME STEEPER HILLS AROUND HERE
RADIO FLYER

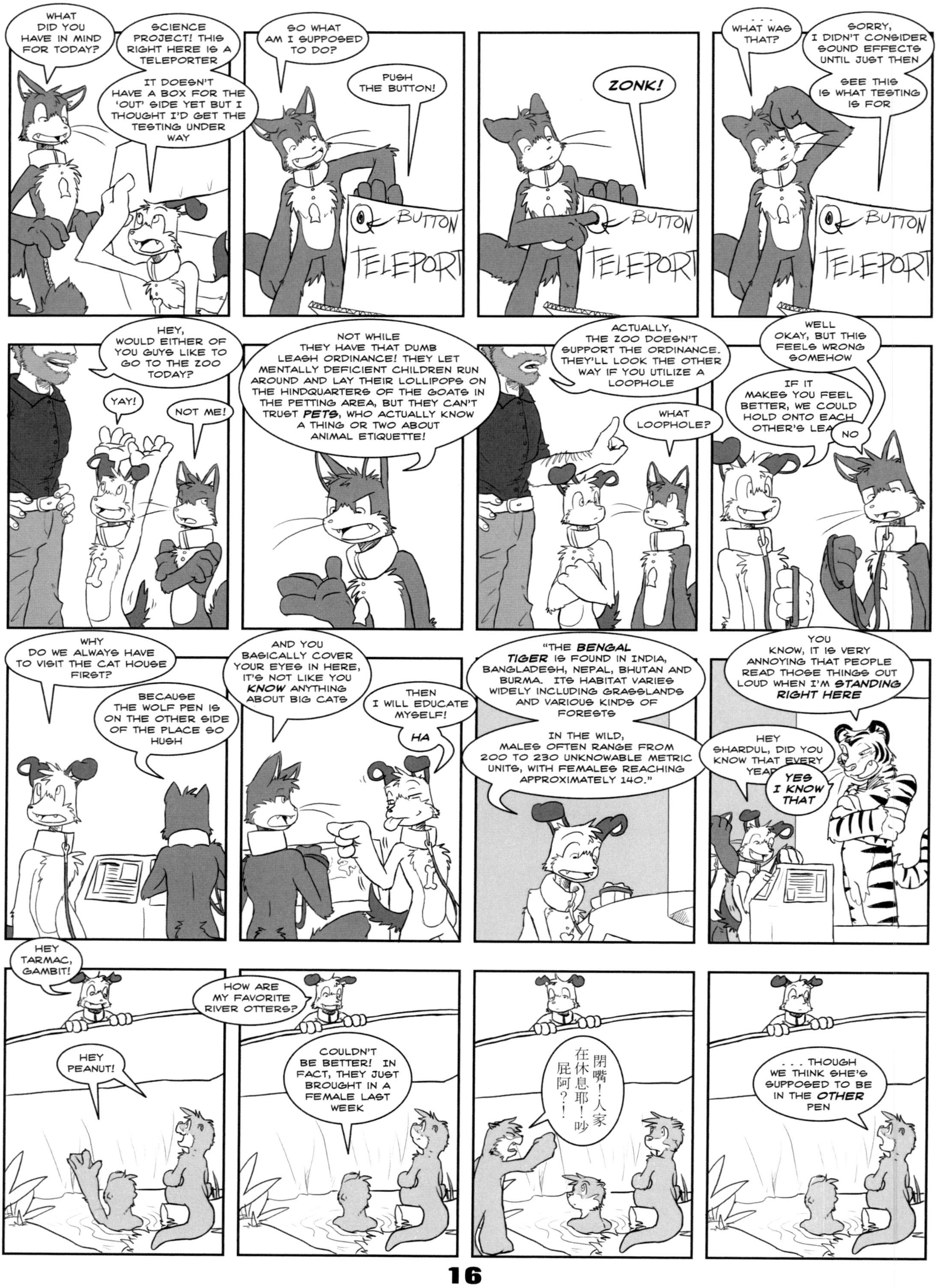
WHAT DID YOU HAVE IN MIND FOR TODAY?
SCIENCE PROJECT! THIS RIGHT HERE IS A TELEPORTER
IT DOESN'T HAVE A BOX FOR THE 'OUT' SIDE YET BUT I THOUGHT I'D GET THE TESTING UNDER WAY
SO WHAT AM I SUPPOSED TO DO?
PUSH THE BUTTON!
BUTTON
TELEPORT
ZONK!
BUTTON
TELEPORT
. . . WHAT WAS THAT?
SORRY, I DIDN'T CONSIDER SOUND EFFECTS UNTIL JUST THEN
SEE THIS IS WHAT TESTING IS FOR
BUTTON
TELEPORT
HEY, WOULD EITHER OF YOU GUYS LIKE TO GO TO THE ZOO TODAY?
YAY!
NOT ME!
NOT WHILE THEY HAVE THAT DUMB LEASH ORDINANCE! THEY LET MENTALLY DEFICIENT CHILDREN RUN AROUND AND LAY THEIR LOLLIPOPS ON THE HINDQUARTERS OF THE GOATS IN THE PETTING AREA, BUT THEY CAN'T TRUST PETS, WHO ACTUALLY KNOW A THING OR TWO ABOUT ANIMAL ETIQUETTE!
ACTUALLY, THE ZOO DOESN'T SUPPORT THE ORDINANCE. THEY'LL LOOK THE OTHER WAY IF YOU UTILIZE A LOOPHOLE
WHAT LOOPHOLE?
WELL OKAY, BUT THIS FEELS WRONG SOMEHOW
IF IT MAKES YOU FEEL BETTER, WE COULD HOLD ONTO EACH OTHER'S LEA
NO
WHY DO WE ALWAYS HAVE TO VISIT THE CAT HOUSE FIRST?
BECAUSE THE WOLF PEN IS ON THE OTHER SIDE OF THE PLACE SO HUSH
AND YOU BASICALLY COVER YOUR EYES IN HERE, IT'S NOT LIKE YOU KNOW ANYTHING ABOUT BIG CATS
THEN I WILL EDUCATE MYSELF!
HA
"THE BENGAL TIGER IS FOUND IN INDIA, BANGLADESH, NEPAL, BHUTAN AND BURMA. ITS HABITAT VARIES WIDELY INCLUDING GRASSLANDS AND VARIOUS KINDS OF FORESTS
IN THE WILD, MALES OFTEN RANGE FROM 200 TO 230 UNKNOWABLE METRIC UNITS, WITH FEMALES REACHING APPROXIMATELY 140."
YOU KNOW, IT IS VERY ANNOYING THAT PEOPLE READ THOSE THINGS OUT LOUD WHEN I'M STANDING RIGHT HERE
HEY SHARDUL, DID YOU KNOW THAT EVERY YEA
YES I KNOW THAT
HEY TARMAC, GAMBIT!
HEY PEANUT!
HOW ARE MY FAVORITE RIVER OTTERS?
COULDN'T BE BETTER! IN FACT, THEY JUST BROUGHT IN A FEMALE LAST WEEK
閉嘴！人家在休息耶！吵屁阿？！
. . . THOUGH WE THINK SHE'S SUPPOSED TO BE IN THE OTHER PEN

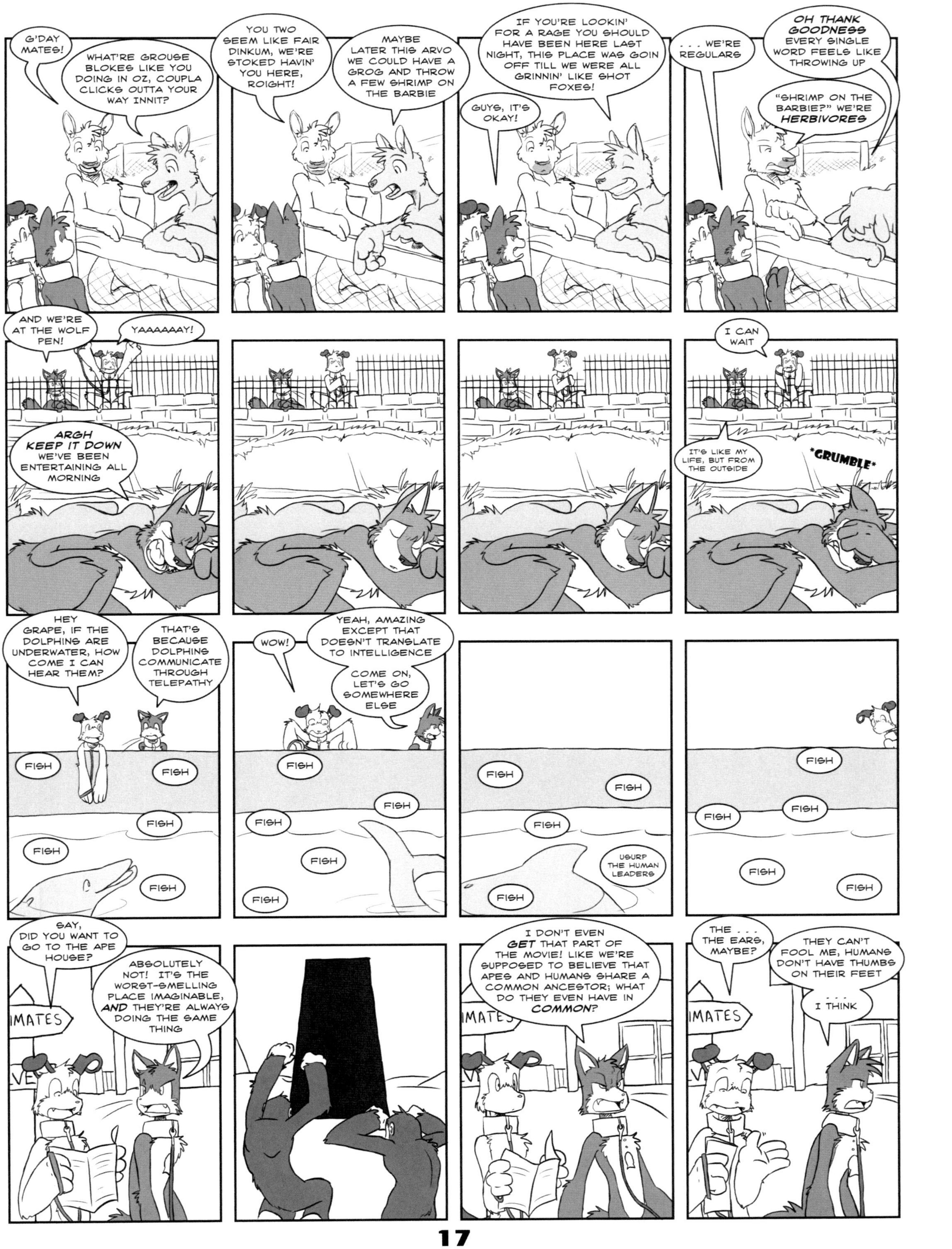
G'DAY MATES!
WHAT'RE GROUSE BLOKES LIKE YOU DOING IN OZ, COUPLA CLICKS OUTTA YOUR WAY INNIT?
YOU TWO SEEM LIKE FAIR DINKUM, WE'RE STOKED HAVIN' YOU HERE, ROIGHT!
MAYBE LATER THIS ARVO WE COULD HAVE A GROG AND THROW A FEW SHRIMP ON THE BARBIE
IF YOU'RE LOOKIN' FOR A RAGE YOU SHOULD HAVE BEEN HERE LAST NIGHT, THIS PLACE WAS GOIN OFF TILL WE WERE ALL GRINNIN' LIKE SHOT FOXES!
GUYS, IT'S OKAY!
. . . WE'RE REGULARS
OH THANK GOODNESS EVERY SINGLE WORD FEELS LIKE THROWING UP
"SHRIMP ON THE BARBIE?" WE'RE HERBIVORES
AND WE'RE AT THE WOLF PEN!
YAAAAAAY!
ARGH KEEP IT DOWN WE'VE BEEN ENTERTAINING ALL MORNING
I CAN WAIT
IT'S LIKE MY LIFE, BUT FROM THE OUTSIDE
GRUMBLE
HEY GRAPE, IF THE DOLPHINS ARE UNDERWATER, HOW COME I CAN HEAR THEM?
THAT'S BECAUSE DOLPHINS COMMUNICATE THROUGH TELEPATHY
FISH
FISH
FISH
FISH
FISH
WOW!
YEAH, AMAZING EXCEPT THAT DOESN'T TRANSLATE TO INTELLIGENCE
COME ON, LET'S GO SOMEWHERE ELSE
FISH
FISH
FISH
FISH
FISH
FISH
FISH
FISH
USURP THE HUMAN LEADERS
FISH
FISH
FISH
FISH
FISH
FISH
SAY, DID YOU WANT TO GO TO THE APE HOUSE?
ABSOLUTELY NOT! IT'S THE WORST-SMELLING PLACE IMAGINABLE, AND THEY'RE ALWAYS DOING THE SAME THING
IMATES
I DON'T EVEN GET THAT PART OF THE MOVIE! LIKE WE'RE SUPPOSED TO BELIEVE THAT APES AND HUMANS SHARE A COMMON ANCESTOR; WHAT DO THEY EVEN HAVE IN COMMON?
IMATES
THE . . . THE EARS, MAYBE?
THEY CAN'T FOOL ME, HUMANS DON'T HAVE THUMBS ON THEIR FEET
. . . I THINK
IMATES

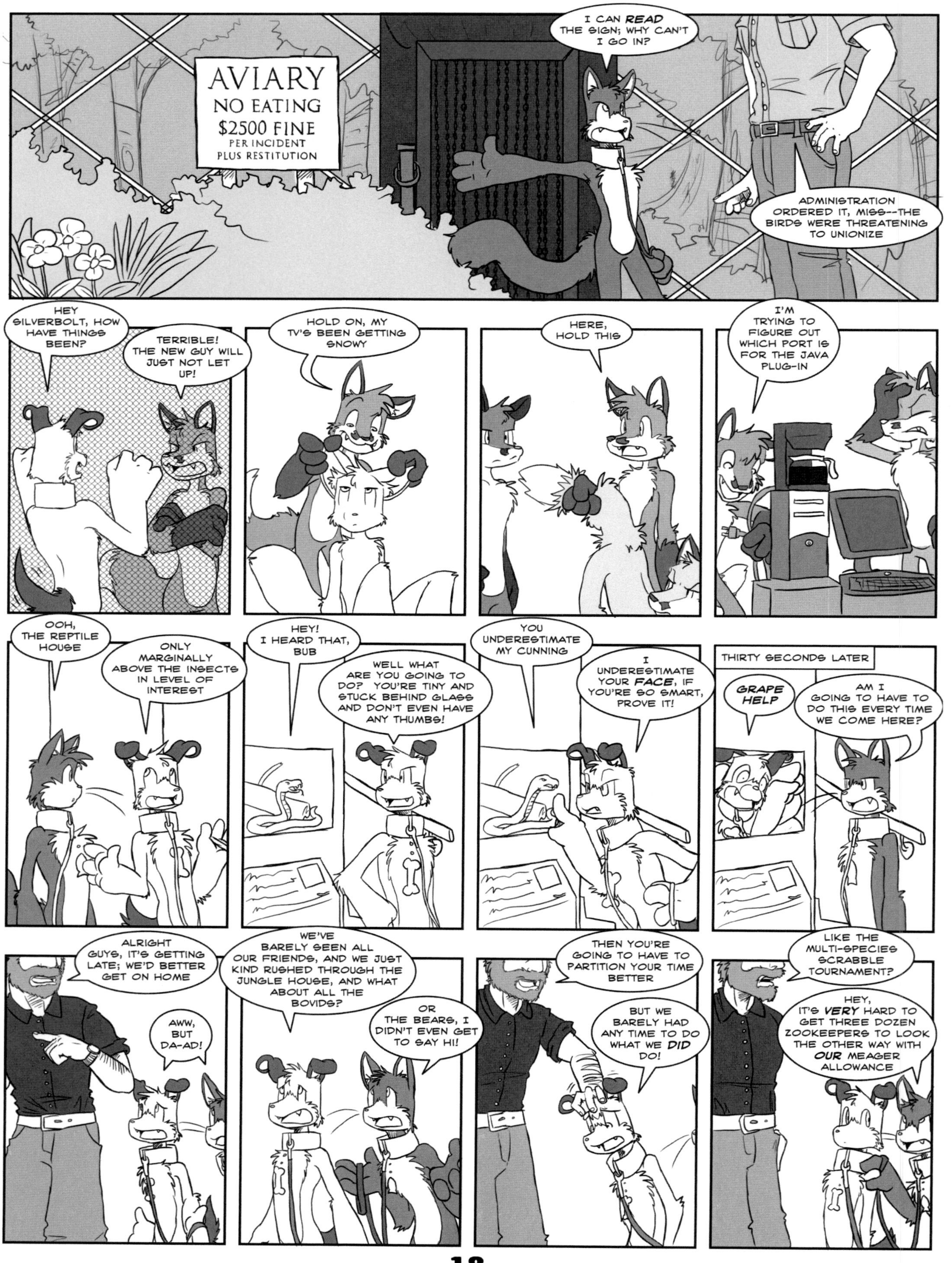
AVIARY
NO EATING
$2500 FINE
PER INCIDENT
PLUS RESTITUTION
I CAN READ THE SIGN; WHY CAN'T I GO IN?
ADMINISTRATION ORDERED IT, MISS--THE BIRDS WERE THREATENING TO UNIONIZE
HEY SILVERBOLT, HOW HAVE THINGS BEEN?
TERRIBLE! THE NEW GUY WILL JUST NOT LET UP!
HOLD ON, MY TV'S BEEN GETTING SNOWY
HERE, HOLD THIS
I'M TRYING TO FIGURE OUT WHICH PORT IS FOR THE JAVA PLUG-IN
OOH, THE REPTILE HOUSE
ONLY MARGINALLY ABOVE THE INSECTS IN LEVEL OF INTEREST
HEY! I HEARD THAT, BUB
WELL WHAT ARE YOU GOING TO DO? YOU'RE TINY AND STUCK BEHIND GLASS AND DON'T EVEN HAVE ANY THUMBS!
YOU UNDERESTIMATE MY CUNNING
I UNDERESTIMATE YOUR FACE, IF YOU'RE SO SMART, PROVE IT!
THIRTY SECONDS LATER
GRAPE HELP
AM I GOING TO HAVE TO DO THIS EVERY TIME WE COME HERE?
ALRIGHT GUYS, IT'S GETTING LATE; WE'D BETTER GET ON HOME
AWW, BUT DA-AD!
WE'VE BARELY SEEN ALL OUR FRIENDS, AND WE JUST KIND RUSHED THROUGH THE JUNGLE HOUSE, AND WHAT ABOUT ALL THE BOVIDS?
OR THE BEARS, I DIDN'T EVEN GET TO SAY HI!
THEN YOU'RE GOING TO HAVE TO PARTITION YOUR TIME BETTER
BUT WE BARELY HAD ANY TIME TO DO WHAT WE DID DO!
LIKE THE MULTI-SPECIES SCRABBLE TOURNAMENT?
HEY, IT'S VERY HARD TO GET THREE DOZEN ZOOKEEPERS TO LOOK THE OTHER WAY WITH OUR MEAGER ALLOWANCE

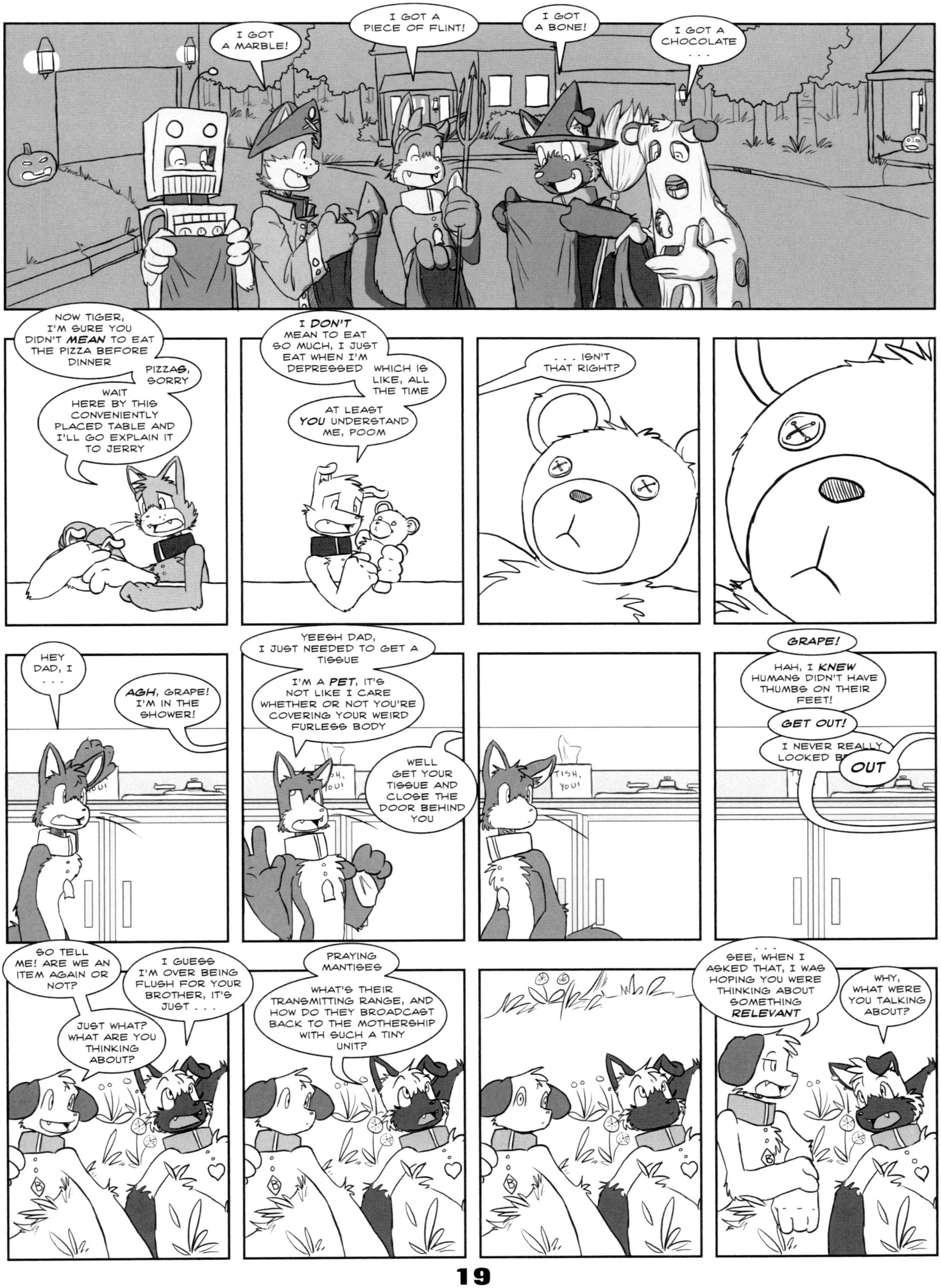
I GOT A MARBLE!
I GOT A PIECE OF FLINT!
I GOT A BONE!
I GOT A CHOCOLATE . . .
NOW TIGER, I'M SURE YOU DIDN'T MEAN TO EAT THE PIZZA BEFORE DINNER
PIZZAS, SORRY
WAIT HERE BY THIS CONVENIENTLY PLACED TABLE AND I'LL GO EXPLAIN IT TO JERRY
I DON'T MEAN TO EAT SO MUCH, I JUST EAT WHEN I'M DEPRESSED
WHICH IS LIKE, ALL THE TIME
AT LEAST YOU UNDERSTAND ME, POOM
. . . ISN'T THAT RIGHT?
HEY DAD, I . . .
AGH, GRAPE! I'M IN THE SHOWER!
YEESH DAD, I JUST NEEDED TO GET A TISSUE
I'M A PET, IT'S NOT LIKE I CARE WHETHER OR NOT YOU'RE COVERING YOUR WEIRD FURLESS BODY
WELL GET YOUR TISSUE AND CLOSE THE DOOR BEHIND YOU
GRAPE!
HAH, I KNEW HUMANS DIDN'T HAVE THUMBS ON THEIR FEET!
GET OUT!
I NEVER REALLY LOOKED B
OUT
SO TELL ME! ARE WE AN ITEM AGAIN OR NOT?
I GUESS I'M OVER BEING FLUSH FOR YOUR BROTHER, IT'S JUST . . .
JUST WHAT? WHAT ARE YOU THINKING ABOUT?
PRAYING MANTISES
WHAT'S THEIR TRANSMITTING RANGE, AND HOW DO THEY BROADCAST BACK TO THE MOTHERSHIP WITH SUCH A TINY UNIT?
. . . SEE, WHEN I ASKED THAT, I WAS HOPING YOU WERE THINKING ABOUT SOMETHING RELEVANT
WHY, WHAT WERE YOU TALKING ABOUT?

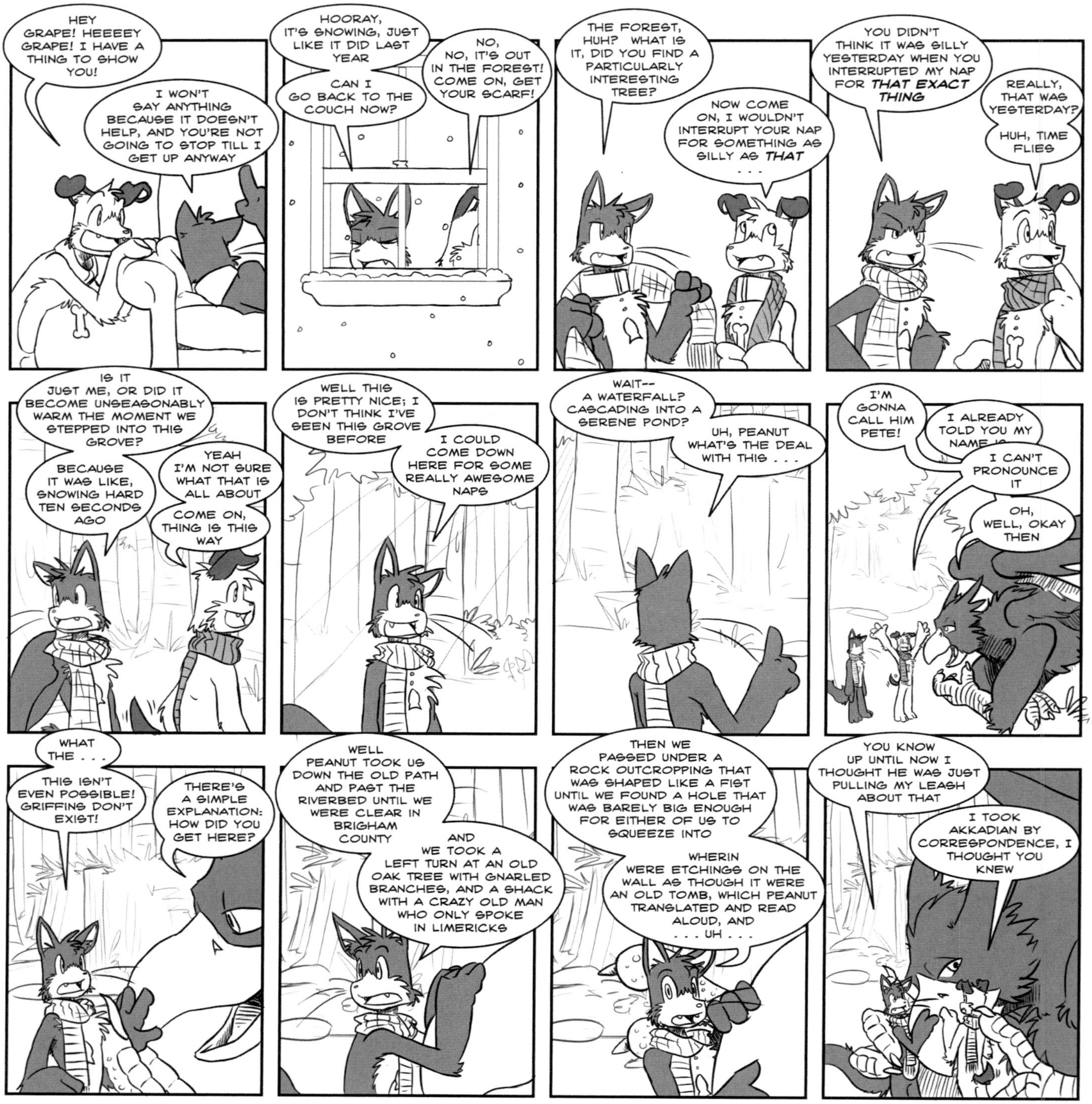
HEY GRAPE! HEEEEY GRAPE! I HAVE A THING TO SHOW YOU!
I WON'T SAY ANYTHING BECAUSE IT DOESN'T HELP, AND YOU'RE NOT GOING TO STOP TILL I GET UP ANYWAY
HOORAY, IT'S SNOWING, JUST LIKE IT DID LAST YEAR
CAN I GO BACK TO THE COUCH NOW?
NO, NO, IT'S OUT IN THE FOREST! COME ON, GET YOUR SCARF!
THE FOREST, HUH? WHAT IS IT, DID YOU FIND A PARTICULARLY INTERESTING TREE?
NOW COME ON, I WOULDN'T INTERRUPT YOUR NAP FOR SOMETHING AS SILLY AS *THAT* . . .
YOU DIDN'T THINK IT WAS SILLY YESTERDAY WHEN YOU INTERRUPTED MY NAP FOR ***THAT EXACT THING***
REALLY, THAT WAS YESTERDAY?
HUH, TIME FLIES
IS IT JUST ME, OR DID IT BECOME UNSEASONABLY WARM THE MOMENT WE STEPPED INTO THIS GROVE?
BECAUSE IT WAS LIKE, SNOWING HARD TEN SECONDS AGO
YEAH I'M NOT SURE WHAT THAT IS ALL ABOUT
COME ON, THING IS THIS WAY
WELL THIS IS PRETTY NICE; I DON'T THINK I'VE SEEN THIS GROVE BEFORE
I COULD COME DOWN HERE FOR SOME REALLY AWESOME NAPS
WAIT-- A WATERFALL? CASCADING INTO A SERENE POND?
UH, PEANUT WHAT'S THE DEAL WITH THIS . . .
I'M GONNA CALL HIM PETE!
I ALREADY TOLD YOU MY NAME IS
I CAN'T PRONOUNCE IT
OH, WELL, OKAY THEN
WHAT THE . . .
THIS ISN'T EVEN POSSIBLE! GRIFFINS DON'T EXIST!
THERE'S A SIMPLE EXPLANATION: HOW DID YOU GET HERE?
WELL PEANUT TOOK US DOWN THE OLD PATH AND PAST THE RIVERBED UNTIL WE WERE CLEAR IN BRIGHAM COUNTY
AND WE TOOK A LEFT TURN AT AN OLD OAK TREE WITH GNARLED BRANCHES, AND A SHACK WITH A CRAZY OLD MAN WHO ONLY SPOKE IN LIMERICKS
THEN WE PASSED UNDER A ROCK OUTCROPPING THAT WAS SHAPED LIKE A FIST UNTIL WE FOUND A HOLE THAT WAS BARELY BIG ENOUGH FOR EITHER OF US TO SQUEEZE INTO
WHERIN WERE ETCHINGS ON THE WALL AS THOUGH IT WERE AN OLD TOMB, WHICH PEANUT TRANSLATED AND READ ALOUD, AND . . . UH . . .
YOU KNOW UP UNTIL NOW I THOUGHT HE WAS JUST PULLING MY LEASH ABOUT THAT
I TOOK AKKADIAN BY CORRESPONDENCE, I THOUGHT YOU KNEW

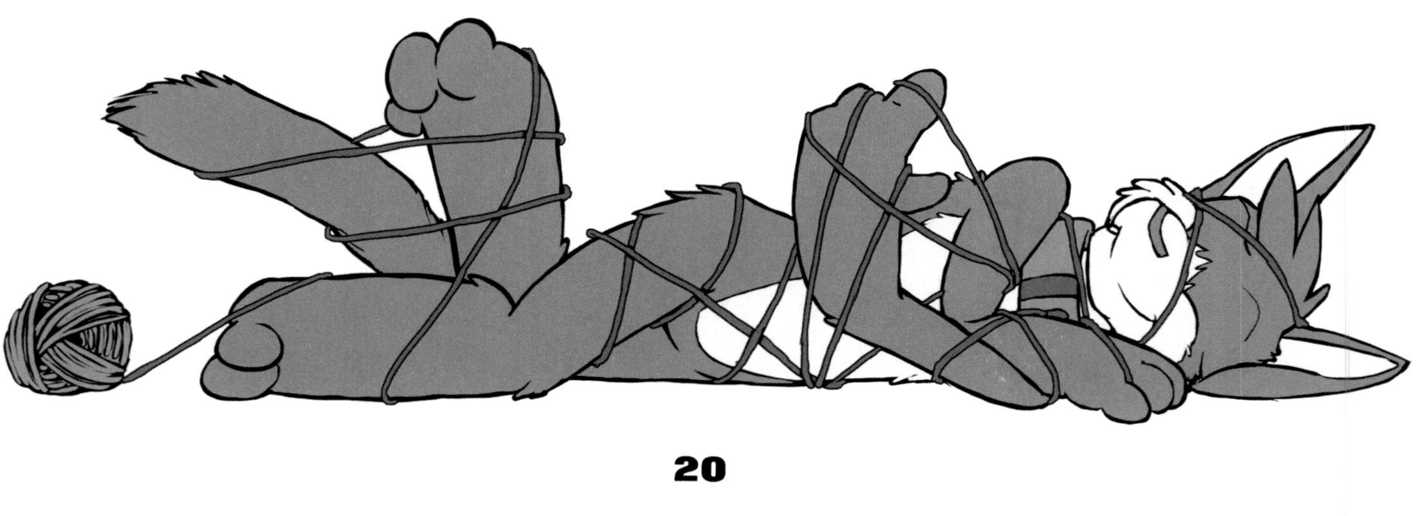

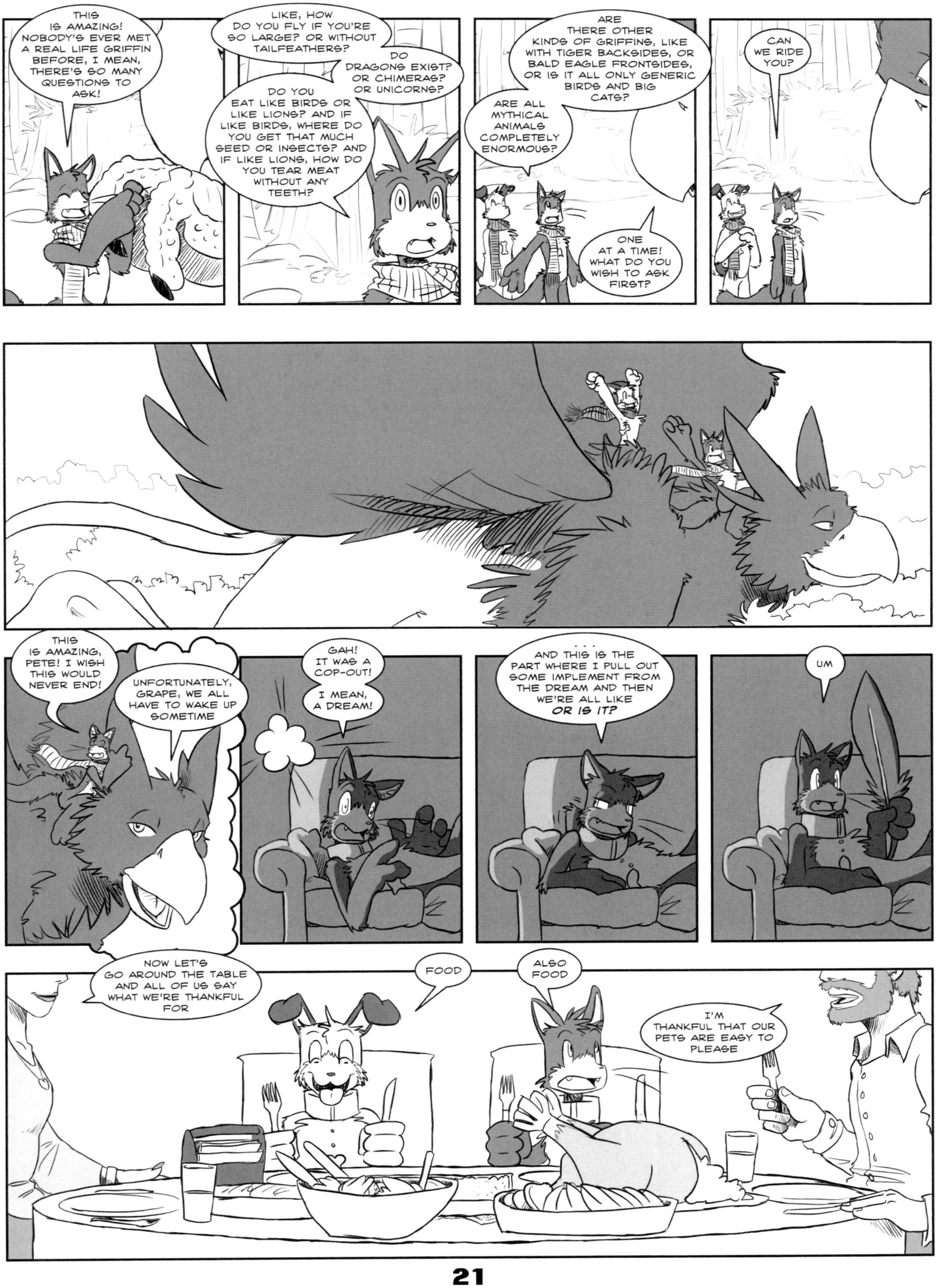

THIS IS AMAZING! NOBODY'S EVER MET A REAL LIFE GRIFFIN BEFORE, I MEAN, THERE'S SO MANY QUESTIONS TO ASK!
LIKE, HOW DO YOU FLY IF YOU'RE SO LARGE? OR WITHOUT TAILFEATHERS?
DO DRAGONS EXIST? OR CHIMERAS? OR UNICORNS?
DO YOU EAT LIKE BIRDS OR LIKE LIONS? AND IF LIKE BIRDS, WHERE DO YOU GET THAT MUCH SEED OR INSECTS? AND IF LIKE LIONS, HOW DO YOU TEAR MEAT WITHOUT ANY TEETH?
ARE THERE OTHER KINDS OF GRIFFINS, LIKE WITH TIGER BACKSIDES, OR BALD EAGLE FRONTSIDES, OR IS IT ALL ONLY GENERIC BIRDS AND BIG CATS?
ARE ALL MYTHICAL ANIMALS COMPLETELY ENORMOUS?
ONE AT A TIME! WHAT DO YOU WISH TO ASK FIRST?
CAN WE RIDE YOU?
THIS IS AMAZING, PETE! I WISH THIS WOULD NEVER END!
UNFORTUNATELY, GRAPE, WE ALL HAVE TO WAKE UP SOMETIME
GAH! IT WAS A COP-OUT!
I MEAN, A DREAM!
...
AND THIS IS THE PART WHERE I PULL OUT SOME IMPLEMENT FROM THE DREAM AND THEN WE'RE ALL LIKE *OR IS IT?*
UM
NOW LET'S GO AROUND THE TABLE AND ALL OF US SAY WHAT WE'RE THANKFUL FOR
FOOD
ALSO FOOD
I'M THANKFUL THAT OUR PETS ARE EASY TO PLEASE

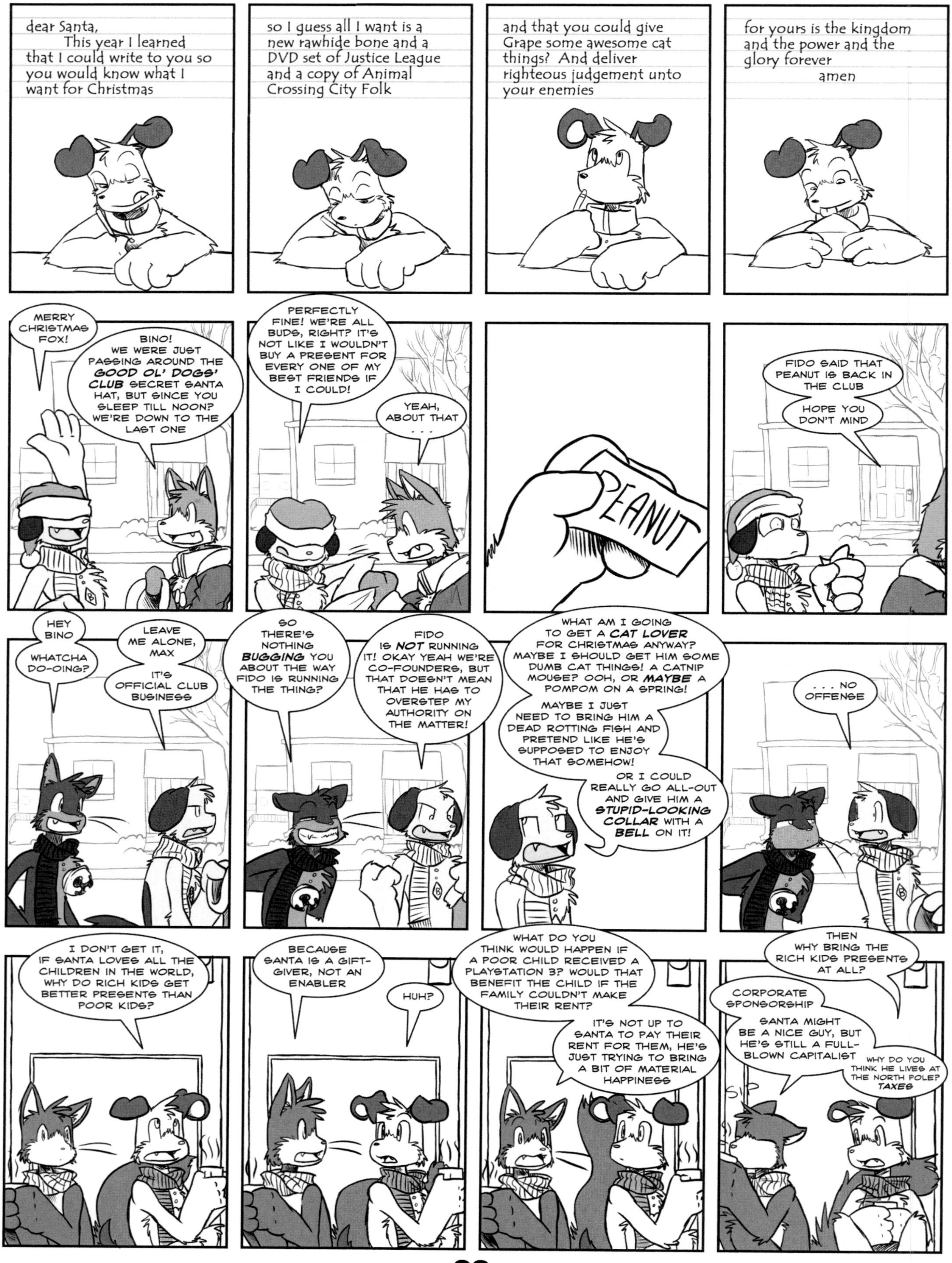
dear Santa,
This year I learned that I could write to you so you would know what I want for Christmas
so I guess all I want is a new rawhide bone and a DVD set of Justice League and a copy of Animal Crossing City Folk
and that you could give Grape some awesome cat things? And deliver righteous judgement unto your enemies
for yours is the kingdom and the power and the glory forever
amen
MERRY CHRISTMAS FOX!
BINO! WE WERE JUST PASSING AROUND THE GOOD OL' DOGS' CLUB SECRET SANTA HAT, BUT SINCE YOU SLEEP TILL NOON? WE'RE DOWN TO THE LAST ONE
PERFECTLY FINE! WE'RE ALL BUDS, RIGHT? IT'S NOT LIKE I WOULDN'T BUY A PRESENT FOR EVERY ONE OF MY BEST FRIENDS IF I COULD!
YEAH, ABOUT THAT . . .
PEANUT
FIDO SAID THAT PEANUT IS BACK IN THE CLUB
HOPE YOU DON'T MIND
HEY BINO
WHATCHA DO-OING?
LEAVE ME ALONE, MAX
IT'S OFFICIAL CLUB BUSINESS
SO THERE'S NOTHING BUGGING YOU ABOUT THE WAY FIDO IS RUNNING THE THING?
FIDO IS NOT RUNNING IT! OKAY YEAH WE'RE CO-FOUNDERS, BUT THAT DOESN'T MEAN THAT HE HAS TO OVERSTEP MY AUTHORITY ON THE MATTER!
WHAT AM I GOING TO GET A CAT LOVER FOR CHRISTMAS ANYWAY? MAYBE I SHOULD GET HIM SOME DUMB CAT THINGS! A CATNIP MOUSE? OOH, OR MAYBE A POMPOM ON A SPRING!
MAYBE I JUST NEED TO BRING HIM A DEAD ROTTING FISH AND PRETEND LIKE HE'S SUPPOSED TO ENJOY THAT SOMEHOW!
OR I COULD REALLY GO ALL-OUT AND GIVE HIM A STUPID-LOOKING COLLAR WITH A BELL ON IT!
. . . NO OFFENSE
I DON'T GET IT, IF SANTA LOVES ALL THE CHILDREN IN THE WORLD, WHY DO RICH KIDS GET BETTER PRESENTS THAN POOR KIDS?
BECAUSE SANTA IS A GIFT-GIVER, NOT AN ENABLER
HUH?
WHAT DO YOU THINK WOULD HAPPEN IF A POOR CHILD RECEIVED A PLAYSTATION 3? WOULD THAT BENEFIT THE CHILD IF THE FAMILY COULDN'T MAKE THEIR RENT?
IT'S NOT UP TO SANTA TO PAY THEIR RENT FOR THEM, HE'S JUST TRYING TO BRING A BIT OF MATERIAL HAPPINESS
THEN WHY BRING THE RICH KIDS PRESENTS AT ALL?
CORPORATE SPONSORSHIP
SANTA MIGHT BE A NICE GUY, BUT HE'S STILL A FULL-BLOWN CAPITALIST
SIP
WHY DO YOU THINK HE LIVES AT THE NORTH POLE? TAXES

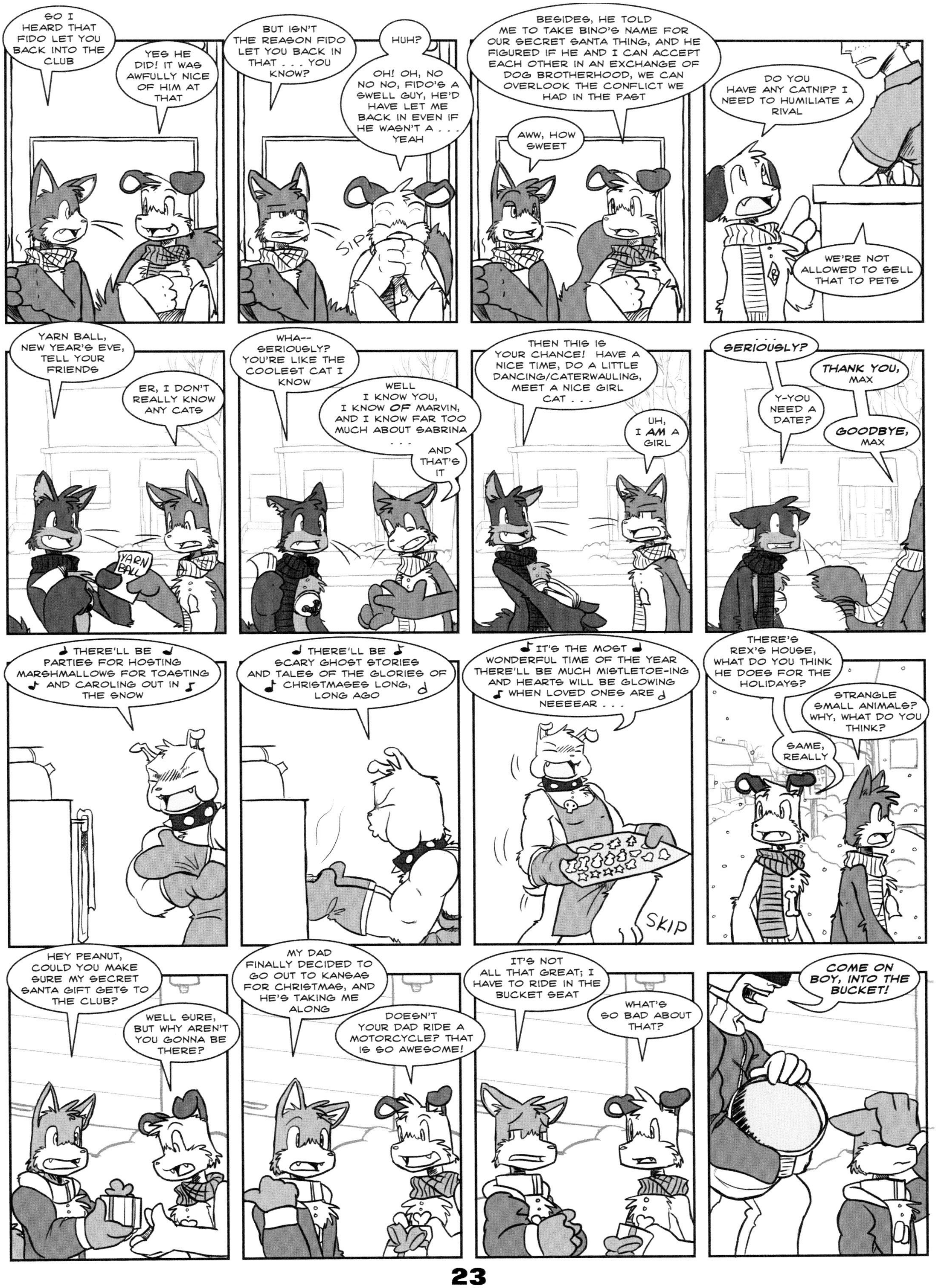
SO I HEARD THAT FIDO LET YOU BACK INTO THE CLUB
YES HE DID! IT WAS AWFULLY NICE OF HIM AT THAT
BUT ISN'T THE REASON FIDO LET YOU BACK IN THAT . . . YOU KNOW?
HUH?
OH! OH, NO NO NO, FIDO'S A SWELL GUY, HE'D HAVE LET ME BACK IN EVEN IF HE WASN'T A . . . YEAH
SIP
BESIDES, HE TOLD ME TO TAKE BINO'S NAME FOR OUR SECRET SANTA THING, AND HE FIGURED IF HE AND I CAN ACCEPT EACH OTHER IN AN EXCHANGE OF DOG BROTHERHOOD, WE CAN OVERLOOK THE CONFLICT WE HAD IN THE PAST
AWW, HOW SWEET
DO YOU HAVE ANY CATNIP? I NEED TO HUMILIATE A RIVAL
WE'RE NOT ALLOWED TO SELL THAT TO PETS
YARN BALL, NEW YEAR'S EVE, TELL YOUR FRIENDS
ER, I DON'T REALLY KNOW ANY CATS
YARN BALL
WHA-- SERIOUSLY? YOU'RE LIKE THE COOLEST CAT I KNOW
WELL I KNOW YOU, I KNOW *OF* MARVIN, AND I KNOW FAR TOO MUCH ABOUT SABRINA . . .
AND THAT'S IT
THEN THIS IS YOUR CHANCE! HAVE A NICE TIME, DO A LITTLE DANCING/CATERWAULING, MEET A NICE GIRL CAT . . .
UH, I *AM* A GIRL
. . . ***SERIOUSLY?***
Y-YOU NEED A DATE?
THANK YOU, MAX
GOODBYE, MAX
THERE'LL BE PARTIES FOR HOSTING MARSHMALLOWS FOR TOASTING AND CAROLING OUT IN THE SNOW
THERE'LL BE SCARY GHOST STORIES AND TALES OF THE GLORIES OF CHRISTMASES LONG, LONG AGO
IT'S THE MOST WONDERFUL TIME OF THE YEAR THERE'LL BE MUCH MISTLETOE-ING AND HEARTS WILL BE GLOWING WHEN LOVED ONES ARE NEEEEAR . . .
SKIP
THERE'S REX'S HOUSE, WHAT DO YOU THINK HE DOES FOR THE HOLIDAYS?
STRANGLE SMALL ANIMALS? WHY, WHAT DO YOU THINK?
SAME, REALLY
HEY PEANUT, COULD YOU MAKE SURE MY SECRET SANTA GIFT GETS TO THE CLUB?
WELL SURE, BUT WHY AREN'T YOU GONNA BE THERE?
MY DAD FINALLY DECIDED TO GO OUT TO KANSAS FOR CHRISTMAS, AND HE'S TAKING ME ALONG
DOESN'T YOUR DAD RIDE A MOTORCYCLE? THAT IS SO AWESOME!
IT'S NOT ALL THAT GREAT; I HAVE TO RIDE IN THE BUCKET SEAT
WHAT'S SO BAD ABOUT THAT?
COME ON BOY, INTO THE BUCKET!

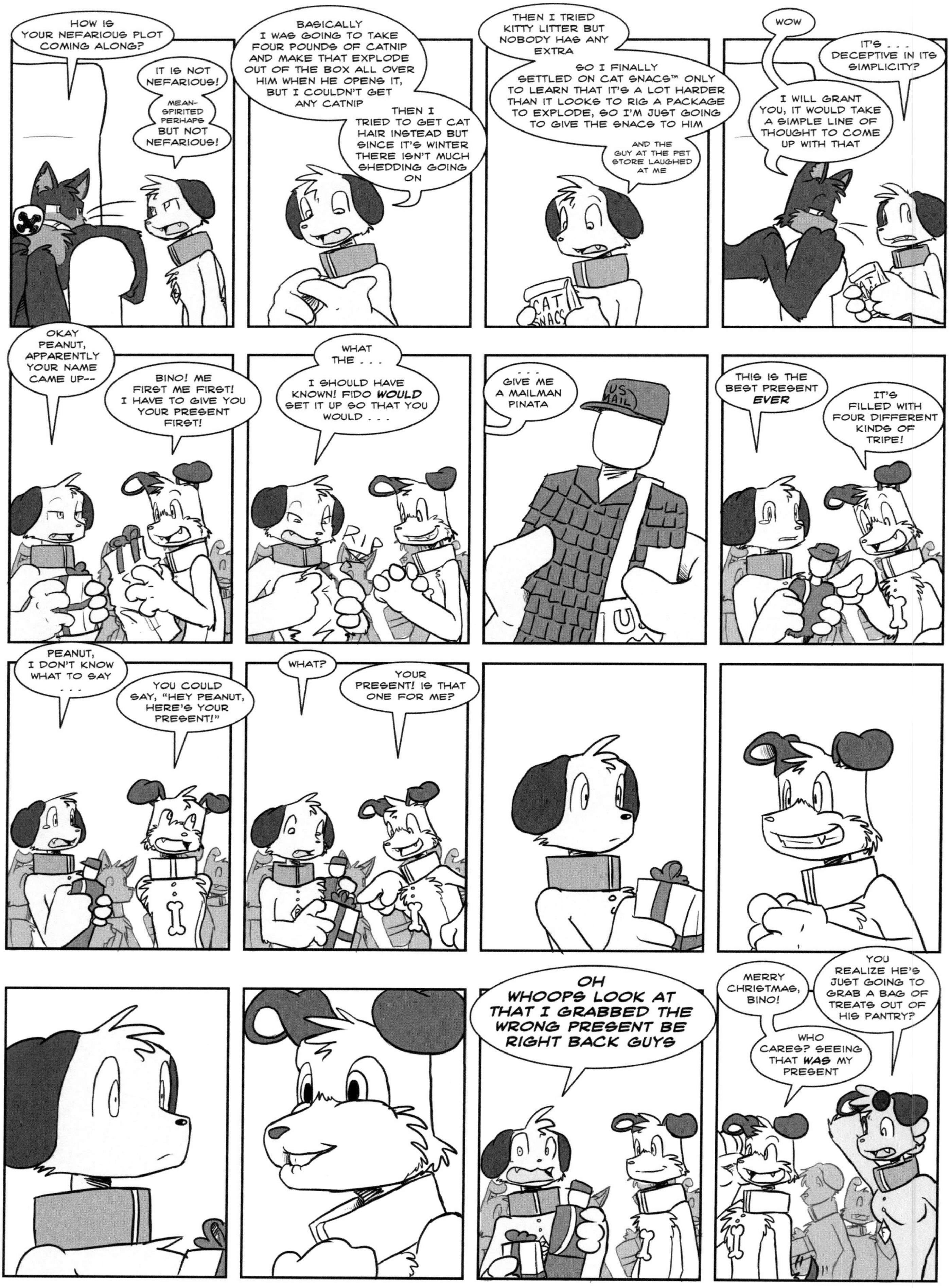
HOW IS YOUR NEFARIOUS PLOT COMING ALONG?
IT IS NOT NEFARIOUS!
MEAN-SPIRITED PERHAPS BUT NOT NEFARIOUS!
BASICALLY I WAS GOING TO TAKE FOUR POUNDS OF CATNIP AND MAKE THAT EXPLODE OUT OF THE BOX ALL OVER HIM WHEN HE OPENS IT, BUT I COULDN'T GET ANY CATNIP
THEN I TRIED TO GET CAT HAIR INSTEAD BUT SINCE IT'S WINTER THERE ISN'T MUCH SHEDDING GOING ON
THEN I TRIED KITTY LITTER BUT NOBODY HAS ANY EXTRA
SO I FINALLY SETTLED ON CAT SNACS™ ONLY TO LEARN THAT IT'S A LOT HARDER THAN IT LOOKS TO RIG A PACKAGE TO EXPLODE, SO I'M JUST GOING TO GIVE THE SNACS TO HIM
AND THE GUY AT THE PET STORE LAUGHED AT ME
CAT SNACS
WOW
IT'S . . . DECEPTIVE IN ITS SIMPLICITY?
I WILL GRANT YOU, IT WOULD TAKE A SIMPLE LINE OF THOUGHT TO COME UP WITH THAT
OKAY PEANUT, APPARENTLY YOUR NAME CAME UP--
BINO! ME FIRST ME FIRST! I HAVE TO GIVE YOU YOUR PRESENT FIRST!
WHAT THE . . .
I SHOULD HAVE KNOWN! FIDO *WOULD* SET IT UP SO THAT YOU WOULD . . .
. . . GIVE ME A MAILMAN PINATA
US MAIL
THIS IS THE BEST PRESENT *EVER*
IT'S FILLED WITH FOUR DIFFERENT KINDS OF TRIPE!
PEANUT, I DON'T KNOW WHAT TO SAY . . .
YOU COULD SAY, "HEY PEANUT, HERE'S YOUR PRESENT!"
WHAT?
YOUR PRESENT! IS THAT ONE FOR ME?
OH WHOOPS LOOK AT THAT I GRABBED THE WRONG PRESENT BE RIGHT BACK GUYS
MERRY CHRISTMAS, BINO!
YOU REALIZE HE'S JUST GOING TO GRAB A BAG OF TREATS OUT OF HIS PANTRY?
WHO CARES? SEEING THAT *WAS* MY PRESENT

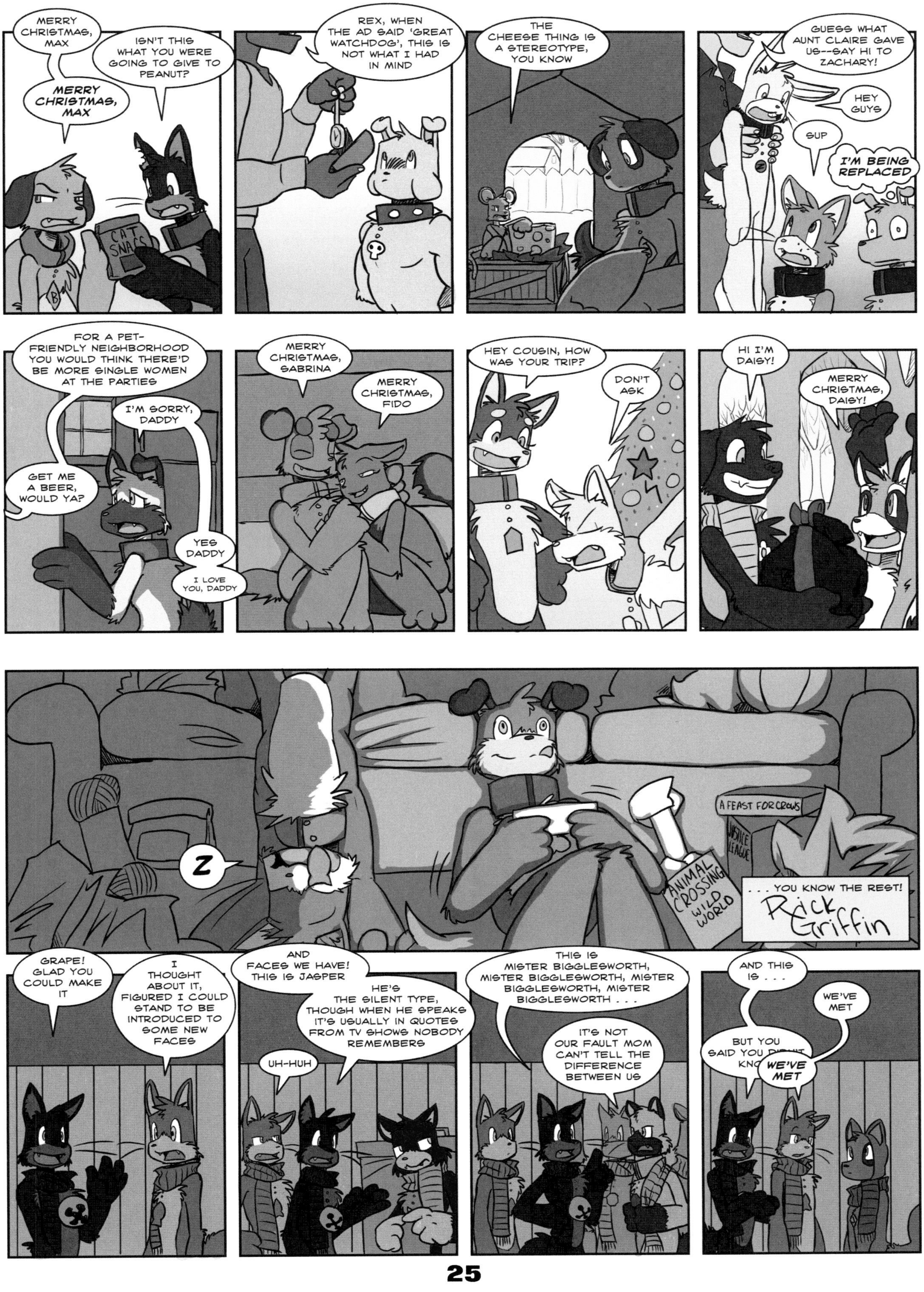
MERRY CHRISTMAS, MAX
MERRY CHRISTMAS, MAX
ISN'T THIS WHAT YOU WERE GOING TO GIVE TO PEANUT?
CAT SNACS
REX, WHEN THE AD SAID 'GREAT WATCHDOG', THIS IS NOT WHAT I HAD IN MIND
THE CHEESE THING IS A STEREOTYPE, YOU KNOW
GUESS WHAT AUNT CLAIRE GAVE US--SAY HI TO ZACHARY!
HEY GUYS
SUP
I'M BEING REPLACED
FOR A PET-FRIENDLY NEIGHBORHOOD YOU WOULD THINK THERE'D BE MORE SINGLE WOMEN AT THE PARTIES
I'M SORRY, DADDY
GET ME A BEER, WOULD YA?
YES DADDY
I LOVE YOU, DADDY
MERRY CHRISTMAS, SABRINA
MERRY CHRISTMAS, FIDO
HEY COUSIN, HOW WAS YOUR TRIP?
DON'T ASK
HI I'M DAISY!
MERRY CHRISTMAS, DAISY!
Z
A FEAST FOR CROWS
JUSTICE LEAGUE
ANIMAL CROSSING WILD WORLD
. . . YOU KNOW THE REST!
Rick Griffin
GRAPE! GLAD YOU COULD MAKE IT
I THOUGHT ABOUT IT, FIGURED I COULD STAND TO BE INTRODUCED TO SOME NEW FACES
AND FACES WE HAVE! THIS IS JASPER
HE'S THE SILENT TYPE, THOUGH WHEN HE SPEAKS IT'S USUALLY IN QUOTES FROM TV SHOWS NOBODY REMEMBERS
UH-HUH
THIS IS MISTER BIGGLESWORTH, MISTER BIGGLESWORTH, MISTER BIGGLESWORTH, MISTER BIGGLESWORTH . . .
IT'S NOT OUR FAULT MOM CAN'T TELL THE DIFFERENCE BETWEEN US
AND THIS IS . . .
WE'VE MET
BUT YOU SAID YOU
WE'VE MET

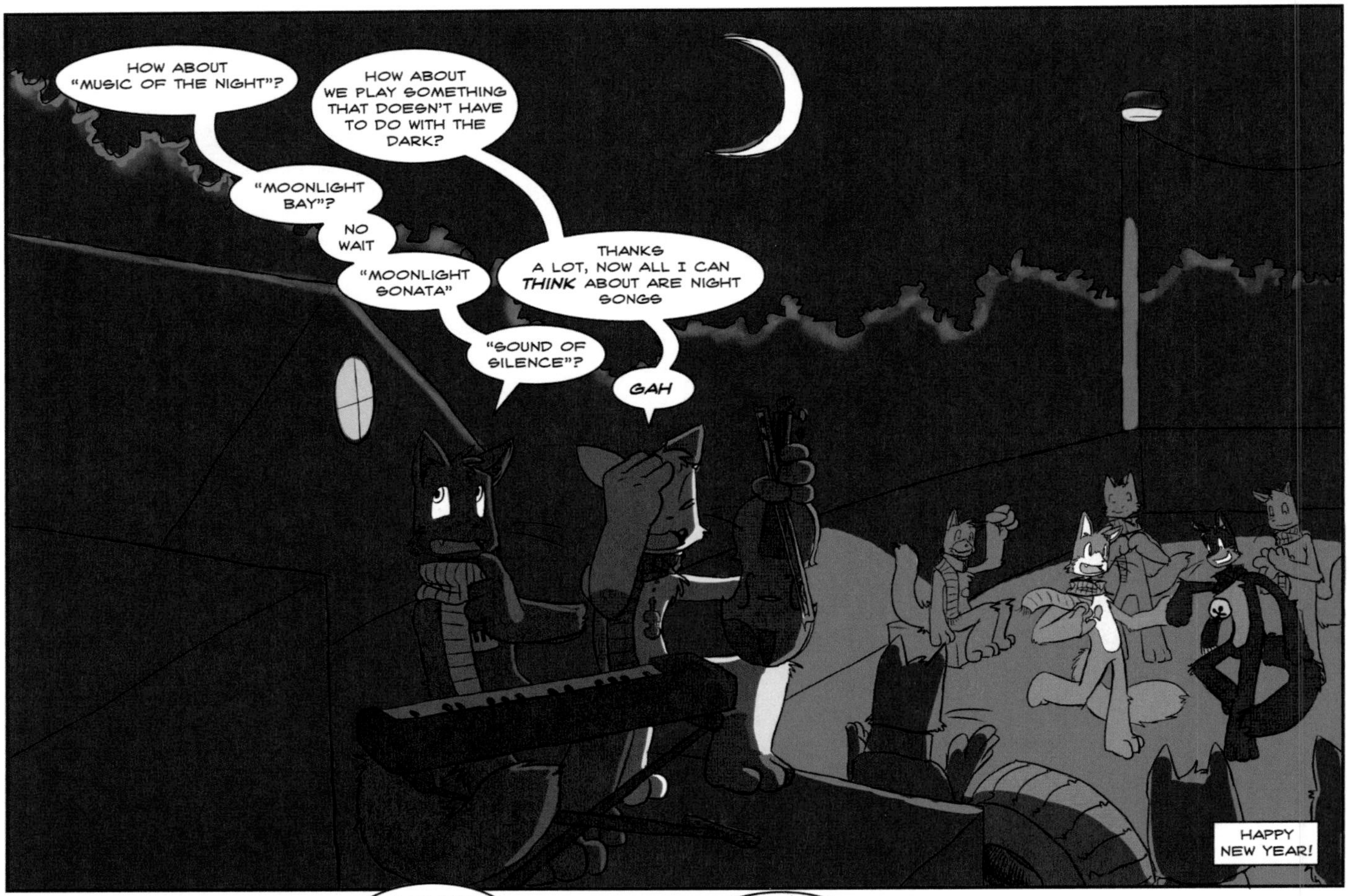
HOW ABOUT "MUSIC OF THE NIGHT"?
HOW ABOUT WE PLAY SOMETHING THAT DOESN'T HAVE TO DO WITH THE DARK?
"MOONLIGHT BAY"?
NO WAIT
"MOONLIGHT SONATA"
THANKS A LOT, NOW ALL I CAN *THINK* ABOUT ARE NIGHT SONGS
"SOUND OF SILENCE"?
GAH
HAPPY NEW YEAR!

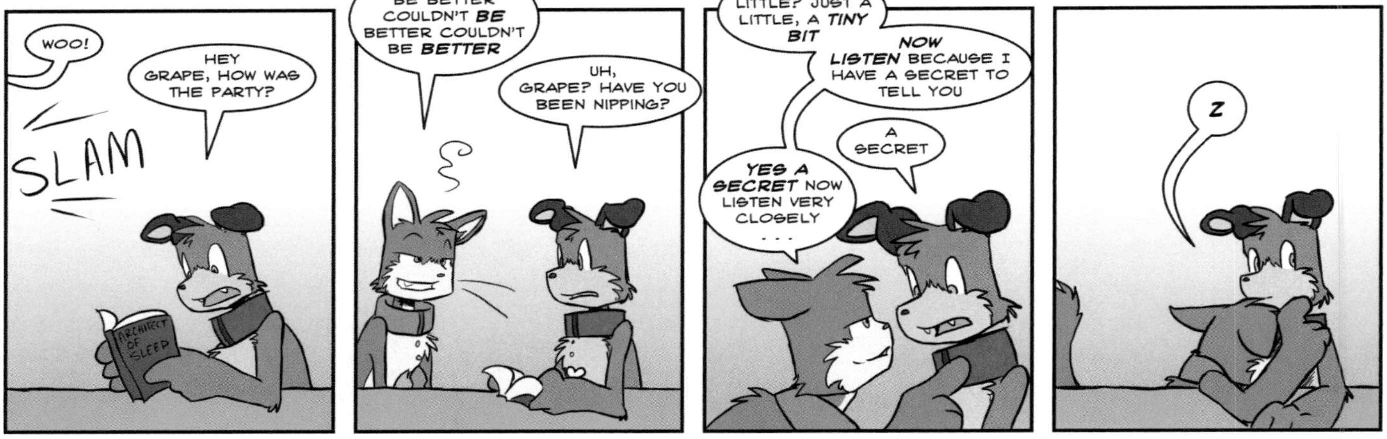
WOO!
SLAM
HEY GRAPE, HOW WAS THE PARTY?
ARCHITECT OF SLEEP
COULDN'T BE BETTER COULDN'T *BE* BETTER COULDN'T BE *BETTER*
UH, GRAPE? HAVE YOU BEEN NIPPING?
A LITTLE? JUST A LITTLE, A *TINY* BIT
NOW LISTEN BECAUSE I HAVE A SECRET TO TELL YOU
A SECRET
YES A SECRET NOW LISTEN VERY CLOSELY . . .
Z

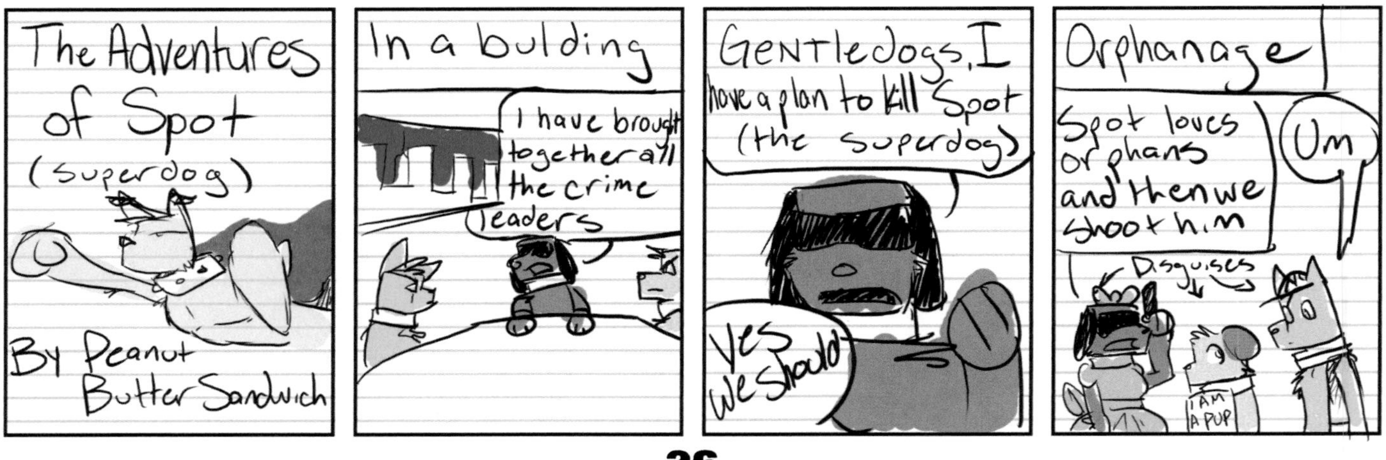
The Adventures of Spot (superdog)
By Peanut Butter Sandwich
In a bulding
I have brought together all the crime leaders
Gentledogs, I have a plan to kill Spot (the superdog)
Yes we should
Orphanage
Spot loves orphans and then we shoot him
Um
Disguises
I AM A PUP

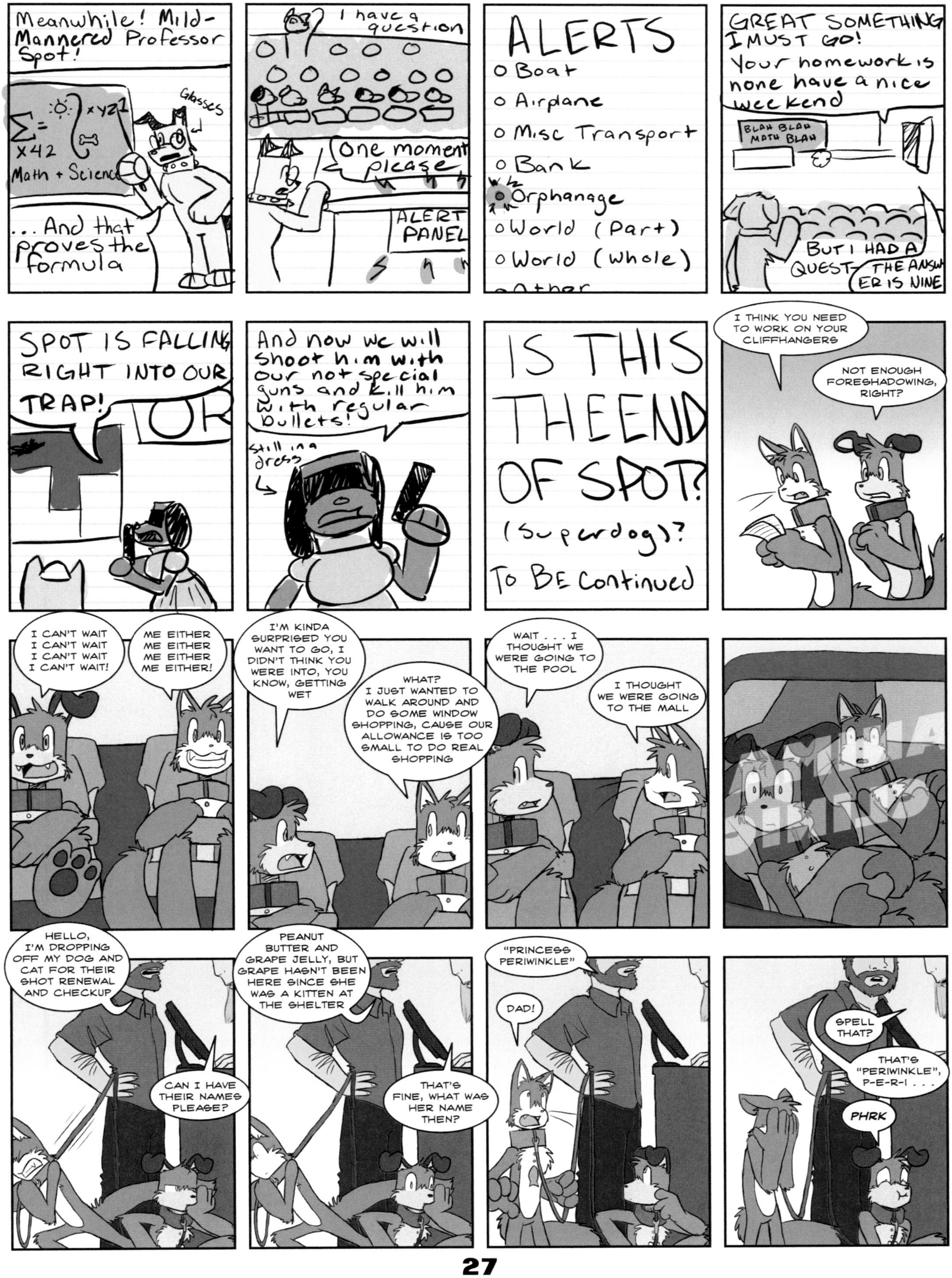
Meanwhile! Mild-Mannered Professor Spot!
Glasses
Math + Science
...And that proves the formula
I have a question
One moment please
ALERT PANEL
ALERTS
o Boat
o Airplane
o Misc Transport
o Bank
Orphanage
o World (Part)
o World (Whole)
GREAT SOMETHING I MUST GO! Your homework is none have a nice weekend
BLAH BLAH MATH BLAH
BUT I HAD A QUEST-
THE ANSWER IS NINE
SPOT IS FALLING RIGHT INTO OUR TRAP!
And now we will shoot him with our not special guns and kill him with regular bullets!
Still in a dress
IS THIS THE END OF SPOT? (Superdog)?
To Be Continued
I THINK YOU NEED TO WORK ON YOUR CLIFFHANGERS
NOT ENOUGH FORESHADOWING, RIGHT?
I CAN'T WAIT I CAN'T WAIT I CAN'T WAIT I CAN'T WAIT!
ME EITHER ME EITHER ME EITHER ME EITHER!
I'M KINDA SURPRISED YOU WANT TO GO, I DIDN'T THINK YOU WERE INTO, YOU KNOW, GETTING WET
WHAT? I JUST WANTED TO WALK AROUND AND DO SOME WINDOW SHOPPING, CAUSE OUR ALLOWANCE IS TOO SMALL TO DO REAL SHOPPING
WAIT . . . I THOUGHT WE WERE GOING TO THE POOL
I THOUGHT WE WERE GOING TO THE MALL
HELLO, I'M DROPPING OFF MY DOG AND CAT FOR THEIR SHOT RENEWAL AND CHECKUP
CAN I HAVE THEIR NAMES PLEASE?
PEANUT BUTTER AND GRAPE JELLY, BUT GRAPE HASN'T BEEN HERE SINCE SHE WAS A KITTEN AT THE SHELTER
THAT'S FINE, WHAT WAS HER NAME THEN?
"PRINCESS PERIWINKLE"
DAD!
SPELL THAT?
THAT'S "PERIWINKLE", P-E-R-I . . .
PHRK

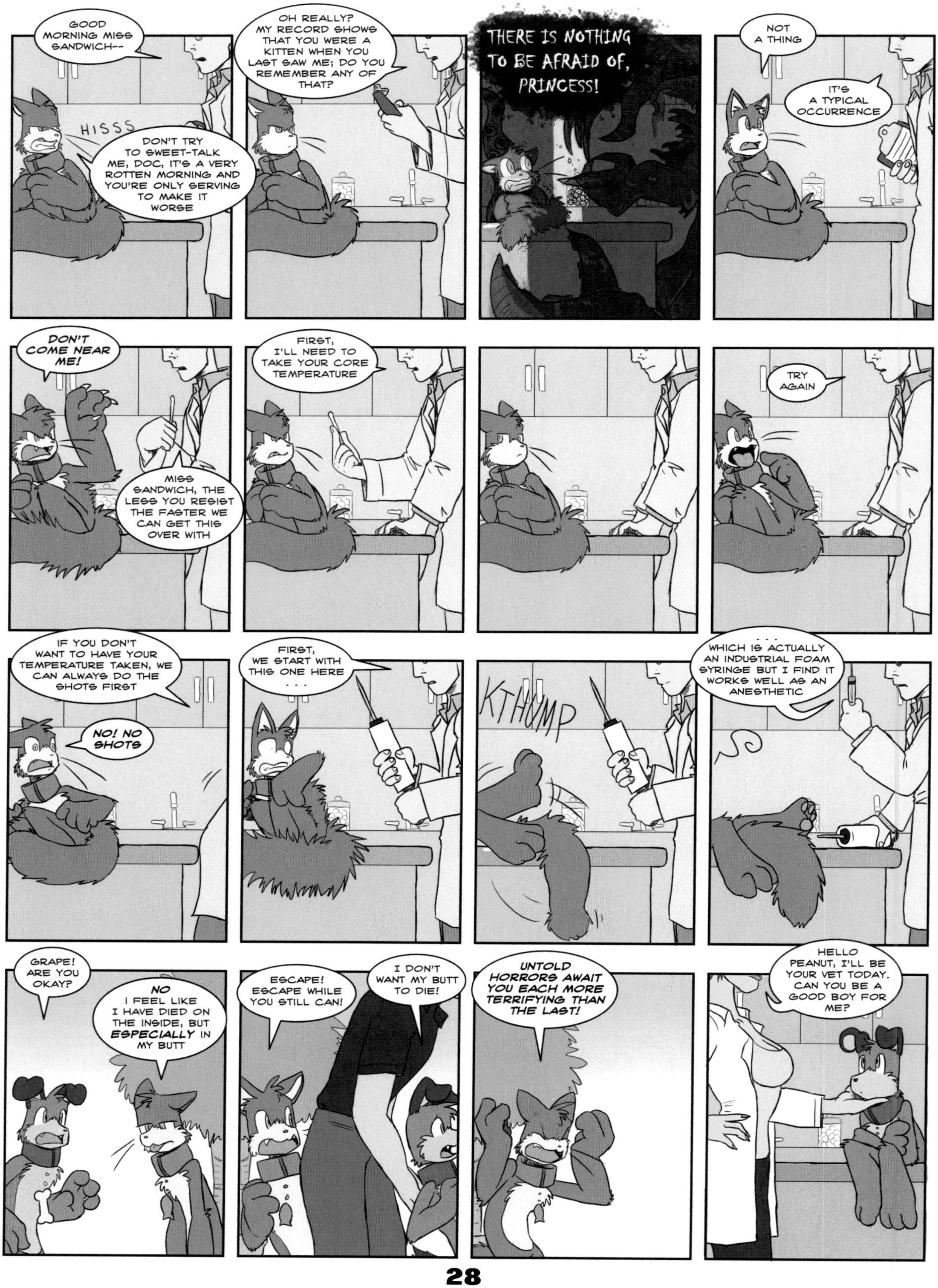
GOOD MORNING MISS SANDWICH--
HISSS
DON'T TRY TO SWEET-TALK ME, DOC, IT'S A VERY ROTTEN MORNING AND YOU'RE ONLY SERVING TO MAKE IT WORSE
OH REALLY? MY RECORD SHOWS THAT YOU WERE A KITTEN WHEN YOU LAST SAW ME; DO YOU REMEMBER ANY OF THAT?
THERE IS NOTHING TO BE AFRAID OF, PRINCESS!
NOT A THING
IT'S A TYPICAL OCCURRENCE
DON'T COME NEAR ME!
MISS SANDWICH, THE LESS YOU RESIST THE FASTER WE CAN GET THIS OVER WITH
FIRST, I'LL NEED TO TAKE YOUR CORE TEMPERATURE
TRY AGAIN
IF YOU DON'T WANT TO HAVE YOUR TEMPERATURE TAKEN, WE CAN ALWAYS DO THE SHOTS FIRST
NO! NO SHOTS
FIRST, WE START WITH THIS ONE HERE . . .
KTHUMP
. . . WHICH IS ACTUALLY AN INDUSTRIAL FOAM SYRINGE BUT I FIND IT WORKS WELL AS AN ANESTHETIC
GRAPE! ARE YOU OKAY?
NO I FEEL LIKE I HAVE DIED ON THE INSIDE, BUT ESPECIALLY IN MY BUTT
ESCAPE! ESCAPE WHILE YOU STILL CAN!
I DON'T WANT MY BUTT TO DIE!
UNTOLD HORRORS AWAIT YOU EACH MORE TERRIFYING THAN THE LAST!
HELLO PEANUT, I'LL BE YOUR VET TODAY. CAN YOU BE A GOOD BOY FOR ME?

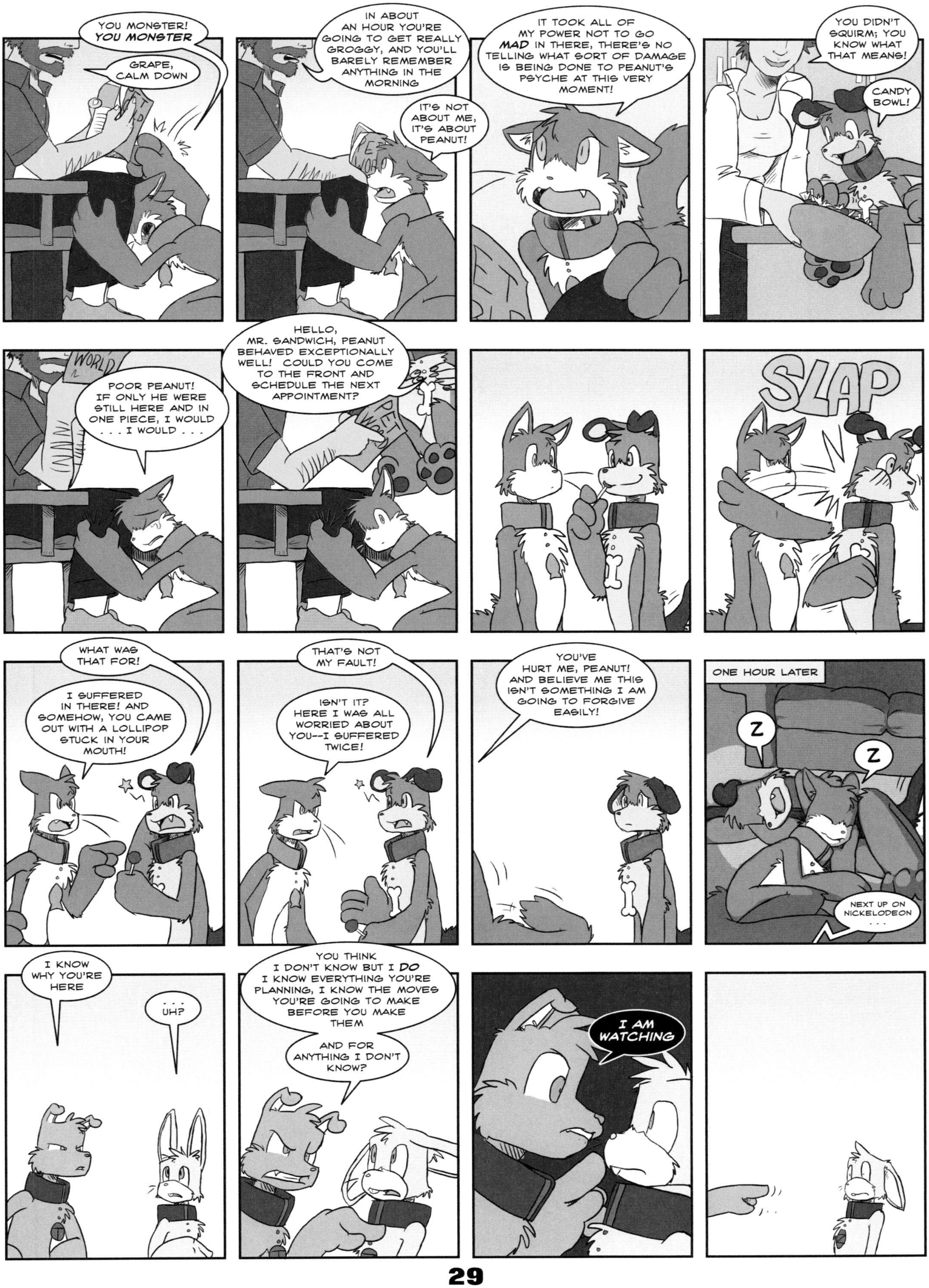

YOU MONSTER! YOU MONSTER
GRAPE, CALM DOWN
IN ABOUT AN HOUR YOU'RE GOING TO GET REALLY GROGGY, AND YOU'LL BARELY REMEMBER ANYTHING IN THE MORNING
IT'S NOT ABOUT ME, IT'S ABOUT PEANUT!
IT TOOK ALL OF MY POWER NOT TO GO MAD IN THERE, THERE'S NO TELLING WHAT SORT OF DAMAGE IS BEING DONE TO PEANUT'S PSYCHE AT THIS VERY MOMENT!
YOU DIDN'T SQUIRM; YOU KNOW WHAT THAT MEANS!
CANDY BOWL!
POOR PEANUT! IF ONLY HE WERE STILL HERE AND IN ONE PIECE, I WOULD . . . I WOULD . . .
HELLO, MR. SANDWICH, PEANUT BEHAVED EXCEPTIONALLY WELL! COULD YOU COME TO THE FRONT AND SCHEDULE THE NEXT APPOINTMENT?
SLAP
WHAT WAS THAT FOR!
I SUFFERED IN THERE! AND SOMEHOW, YOU CAME OUT WITH A LOLLIPOP STUCK IN YOUR MOUTH!
THAT'S NOT MY FAULT!
ISN'T IT? HERE I WAS ALL WORRIED ABOUT YOU--I SUFFERED TWICE!
YOU'VE HURT ME, PEANUT! AND BELIEVE ME THIS ISN'T SOMETHING I AM GOING TO FORGIVE EASILY!
ONE HOUR LATER
Z
Z
NEXT UP ON NICKELODEON . . .
I KNOW WHY YOU'RE HERE
. . . UH?
YOU THINK I DON'T KNOW BUT I DO I KNOW EVERYTHING YOU'RE PLANNING, I KNOW THE MOVES YOU'RE GOING TO MAKE BEFORE YOU MAKE THEM
AND FOR ANYTHING I DON'T KNOW?
I AM WATCHING

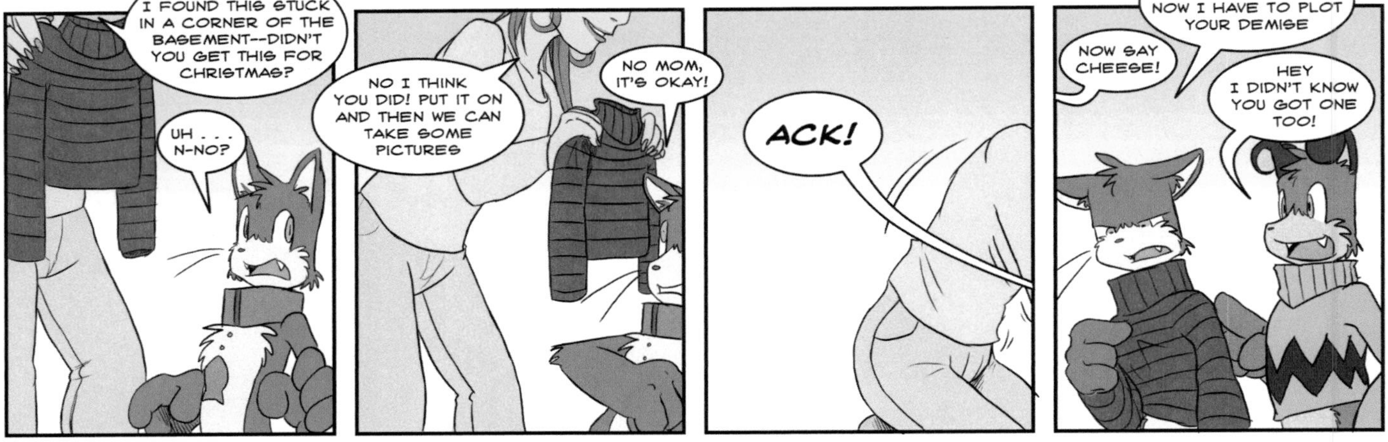
GRAPE! I FOUND THIS STUCK IN A CORNER OF THE BASEMENT--DIDN'T YOU GET THIS FOR CHRISTMAS?
UH . . . N-NO?
NO I THINK YOU DID! PUT IT ON AND THEN WE CAN TAKE SOME PICTURES
NO MOM, IT'S OKAY!
ACK!
NOW SAY CHEESE!
MOM, I LOVE YOU, BUT NOW I HAVE TO PLOT YOUR DEMISE
HEY I DIDN'T KNOW YOU GOT ONE TOO!

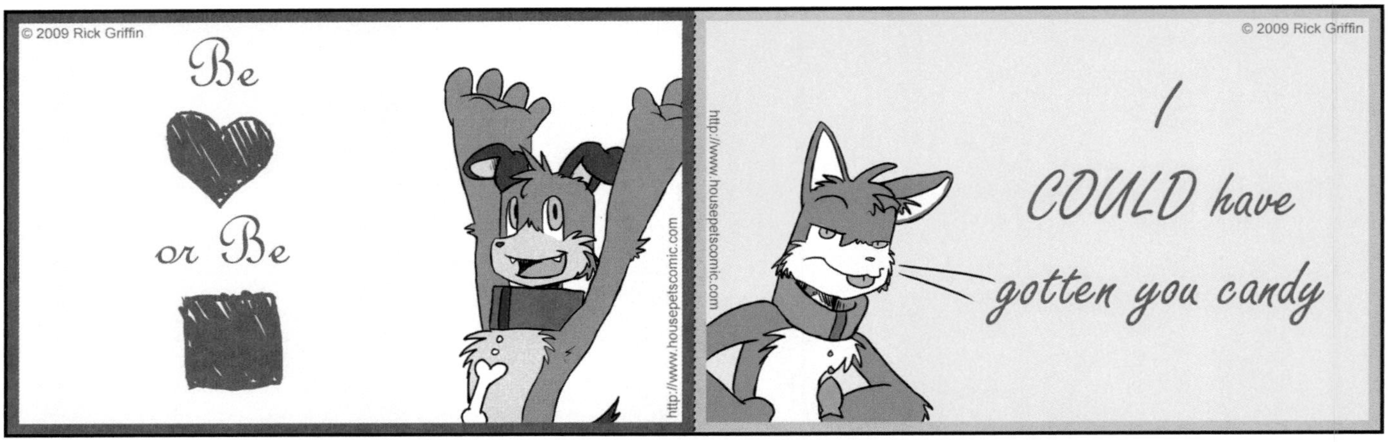
© 2009 Rick Griffin
Be
or Be
http://www.housepetscomic.com
© 2009 Rick Griffin
http://www.housepetscomic.com
I COULD have gotten you candy

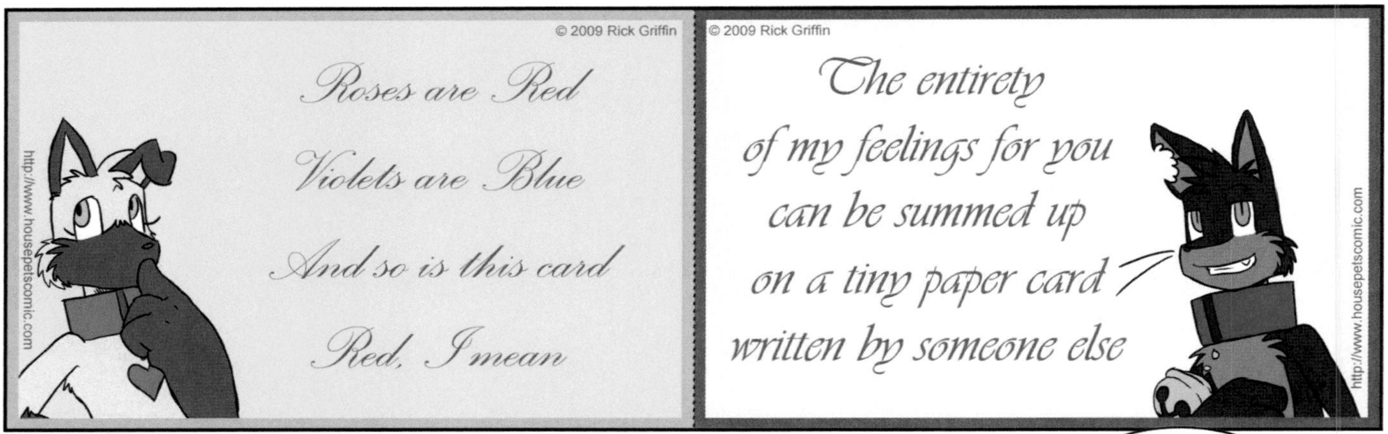
© 2009 Rick Griffin
http://www.housepetscomic.com
Roses are Red
Violets are Blue
And so is this card
Red, I mean
© 2009 Rick Griffin
The entirety of my feelings for you can be summed up on a tiny paper card written by someone else
http://www.housepetscomic.com

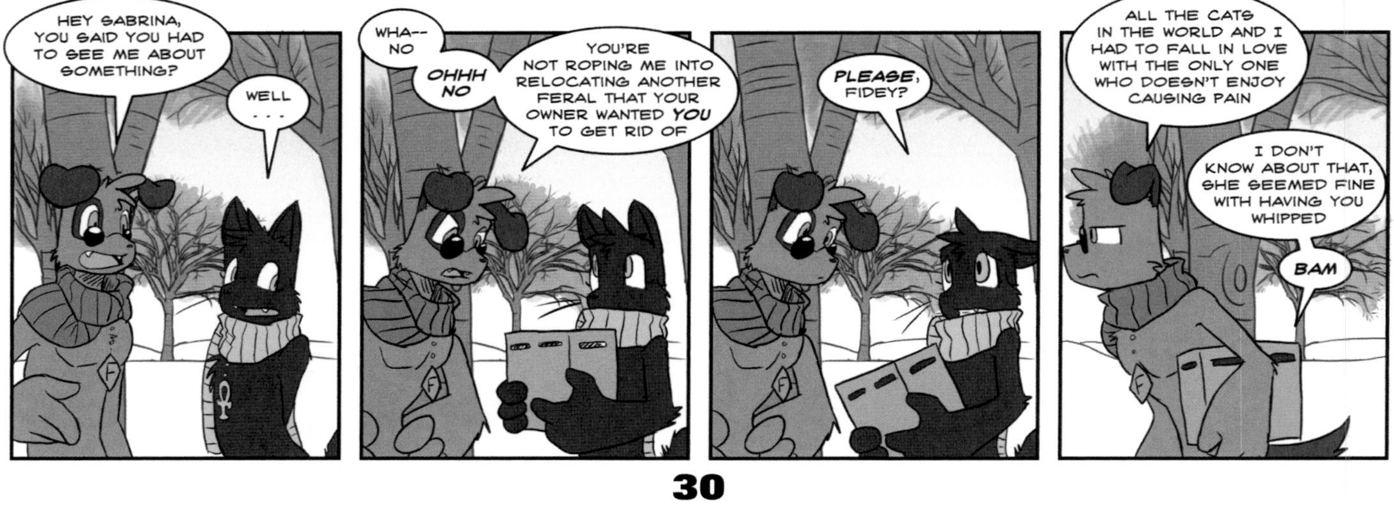
HEY SABRINA, YOU SAID YOU HAD TO SEE ME ABOUT SOMETHING?
WELL . . .
WHA-- NO
OHHH NO
YOU'RE NOT ROPING ME INTO RELOCATING ANOTHER FERAL THAT YOUR OWNER WANTED YOU TO GET RID OF
PLEASE, FIDEY?
ALL THE CATS IN THE WORLD AND I HAD TO FALL IN LOVE WITH THE ONLY ONE WHO DOESN'T ENJOY CAUSING PAIN
I DON'T KNOW ABOUT THAT, SHE SEEMED FINE WITH HAVING YOU WHIPPED
BAM

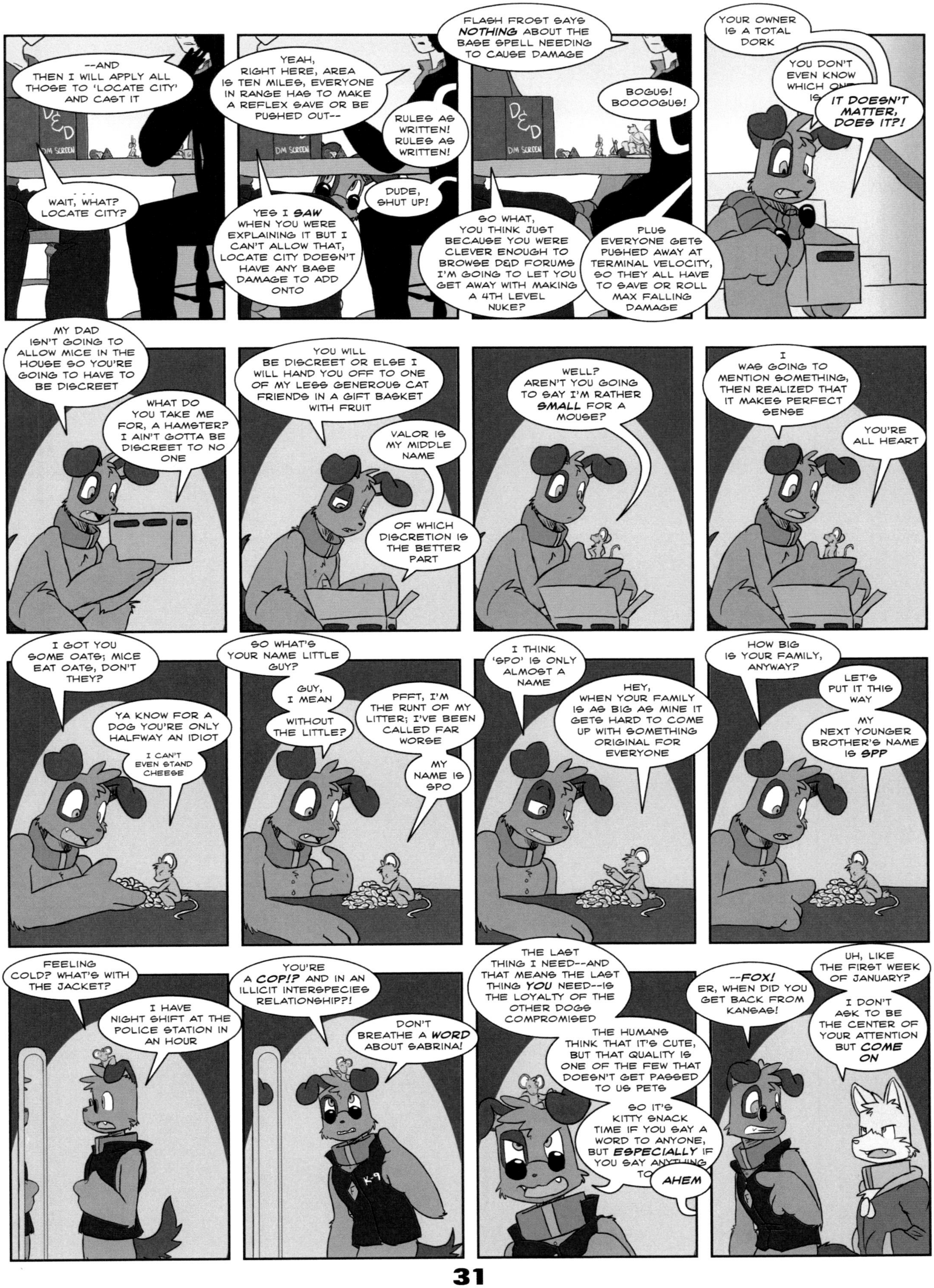
--AND THEN I WILL APPLY ALL THOSE TO 'LOCATE CITY' AND CAST IT
...
WAIT, WHAT? LOCATE CITY?
YEAH, RIGHT HERE, AREA IS TEN MILES, EVERYONE IN RANGE HAS TO MAKE A REFLEX SAVE OR BE PUSHED OUT--
RULES AS WRITTEN! RULES AS WRITTEN!
YES I SAW WHEN YOU WERE EXPLAINING IT BUT I CAN'T ALLOW THAT, LOCATE CITY DOESN'T HAVE ANY BASE DAMAGE TO ADD ONTO
DUDE, SHUT UP!
FLASH FROST SAYS NOTHING ABOUT THE BASE SPELL NEEDING TO CAUSE DAMAGE
BOGUS! BOOOOGUS!
SO WHAT, YOU THINK JUST BECAUSE YOU WERE CLEVER ENOUGH TO BROWSE D&D FORUMS I'M GOING TO LET YOU GET AWAY WITH MAKING A 4TH LEVEL NUKE?
PLUS EVERYONE GETS PUSHED AWAY AT TERMINAL VELOCITY, SO THEY ALL HAVE TO SAVE OR ROLL MAX FALLING DAMAGE
YOUR OWNER IS A TOTAL DORK
YOU DON'T EVEN KNOW WHICH ONE IS
IT DOESN'T MATTER, DOES IT?!
MY DAD ISN'T GOING TO ALLOW MICE IN THE HOUSE SO YOU'RE GOING TO HAVE TO BE DISCREET
WHAT DO YOU TAKE ME FOR, A HAMSTER? I AIN'T GOTTA BE DISCREET TO NO ONE
YOU WILL BE DISCREET OR ELSE I WILL HAND YOU OFF TO ONE OF MY LESS GENEROUS CAT FRIENDS IN A GIFT BASKET WITH FRUIT
VALOR IS MY MIDDLE NAME
OF WHICH DISCRETION IS THE BETTER PART
WELL? AREN'T YOU GOING TO SAY I'M RATHER SMALL FOR A MOUSE?
I WAS GOING TO MENTION SOMETHING, THEN REALIZED THAT IT MAKES PERFECT SENSE
YOU'RE ALL HEART
I GOT YOU SOME OATS; MICE EAT OATS, DON'T THEY?
YA KNOW FOR A DOG YOU'RE ONLY HALFWAY AN IDIOT
I CAN'T EVEN STAND CHEESE
SO WHAT'S YOUR NAME LITTLE GUY?
GUY, I MEAN
WITHOUT THE LITTLE?
PFFT, I'M THE RUNT OF MY LITTER; I'VE BEEN CALLED FAR WORSE
MY NAME IS SPO
I THINK 'SPO' IS ONLY ALMOST A NAME
HEY, WHEN YOUR FAMILY IS AS BIG AS MINE IT GETS HARD TO COME UP WITH SOMETHING ORIGINAL FOR EVERYONE
HOW BIG IS YOUR FAMILY, ANYWAY?
LET'S PUT IT THIS WAY
MY NEXT YOUNGER BROTHER'S NAME IS SPP
FEELING COLD? WHAT'S WITH THE JACKET?
I HAVE NIGHT SHIFT AT THE POLICE STATION IN AN HOUR
YOU'RE A COP!? AND IN AN ILLICIT INTERSPECIES RELATIONSHIP?!
DON'T BREATHE A WORD ABOUT SABRINA!
THE LAST THING I NEED--AND THAT MEANS THE LAST THING YOU NEED--IS THE LOYALTY OF THE OTHER DOGS COMPROMISED
THE HUMANS THINK THAT IT'S CUTE, BUT THAT QUALITY IS ONE OF THE FEW THAT DOESN'T GET PASSED TO US PETS
SO IT'S KITTY SNACK TIME IF YOU SAY A WORD TO ANYONE, BUT ESPECIALLY IF YOU SAY ANYTHING TO
AHEM
--FOX! ER, WHEN DID YOU GET BACK FROM KANSAS!
UH, LIKE THE FIRST WEEK OF JANUARY?
I DON'T ASK TO BE THE CENTER OF YOUR ATTENTION BUT COME ON

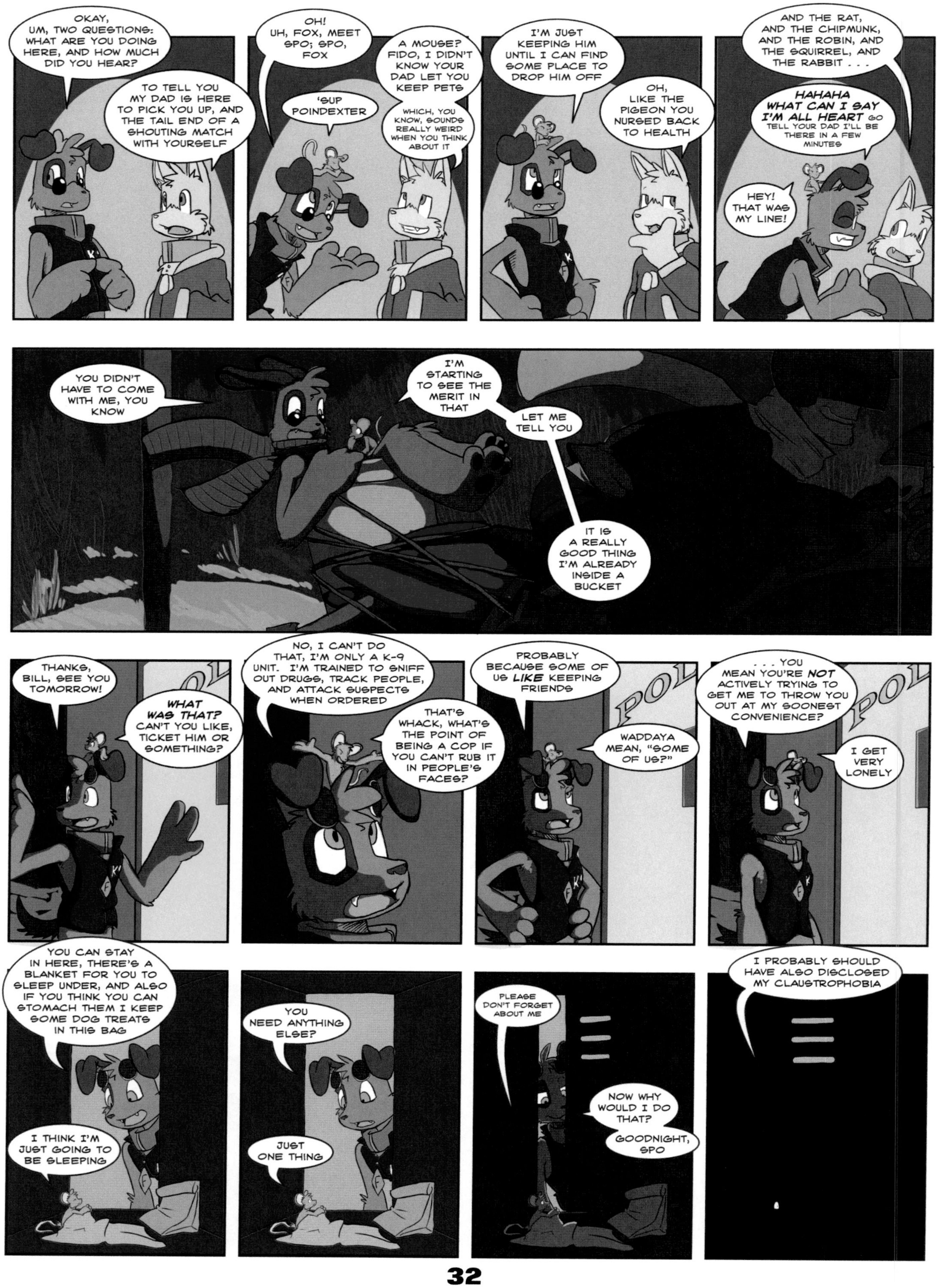
OKAY, UM, TWO QUESTIONS: WHAT ARE YOU DOING HERE, AND HOW MUCH DID YOU HEAR?
TO TELL YOU MY DAD IS HERE TO PICK YOU UP, AND THE TAIL END OF A SHOUTING MATCH WITH YOURSELF
OH! UH, FOX, MEET SPO; SPO, FOX
'SUP POINDEXTER
A MOUSE? FIDO, I DIDN'T KNOW YOUR DAD LET YOU KEEP PETS
WHICH, YOU KNOW, SOUNDS REALLY WEIRD WHEN YOU THINK ABOUT IT
I'M JUST KEEPING HIM UNTIL I CAN FIND SOME PLACE TO DROP HIM OFF
OH, LIKE THE PIGEON YOU NURSED BACK TO HEALTH
AND THE RAT, AND THE CHIPMUNK, AND THE ROBIN, AND THE SQUIRREL, AND THE RABBIT . . .
HAHAHA WHAT CAN I SAY I'M ALL HEART GO TELL YOUR DAD I'LL BE THERE IN A FEW MINUTES
HEY! THAT WAS MY LINE!
YOU DIDN'T HAVE TO COME WITH ME, YOU KNOW
I'M STARTING TO SEE THE MERIT IN THAT
LET ME TELL YOU
IT IS A REALLY GOOD THING I'M ALREADY INSIDE A BUCKET
THANKS, BILL, SEE YOU TOMORROW!
WHAT WAS THAT? CAN'T YOU LIKE, TICKET HIM OR SOMETHING?
NO, I CAN'T DO THAT, I'M ONLY A K-9 UNIT. I'M TRAINED TO SNIFF OUT DRUGS, TRACK PEOPLE, AND ATTACK SUSPECTS WHEN ORDERED
THAT'S WHACK, WHAT'S THE POINT OF BEING A COP IF YOU CAN'T RUB IT IN PEOPLE'S FACES?
PROBABLY BECAUSE SOME OF US LIKE KEEPING FRIENDS
WADDAYA MEAN, "SOME OF US?"
. . . YOU MEAN YOU'RE NOT ACTIVELY TRYING TO GET ME TO THROW YOU OUT AT MY SOONEST CONVENIENCE?
I GET VERY LONELY
YOU CAN STAY IN HERE, THERE'S A BLANKET FOR YOU TO SLEEP UNDER, AND ALSO IF YOU THINK YOU CAN STOMACH THEM I KEEP SOME DOG TREATS IN THIS BAG
I THINK I'M JUST GOING TO BE SLEEPING
YOU NEED ANYTHING ELSE?
JUST ONE THING
PLEASE DON'T FORGET ABOUT ME
NOW WHY WOULD I DO THAT?
GOODNIGHT, SPO
I PROBABLY SHOULD HAVE ALSO DISCLOSED MY CLAUSTROPHOBIA

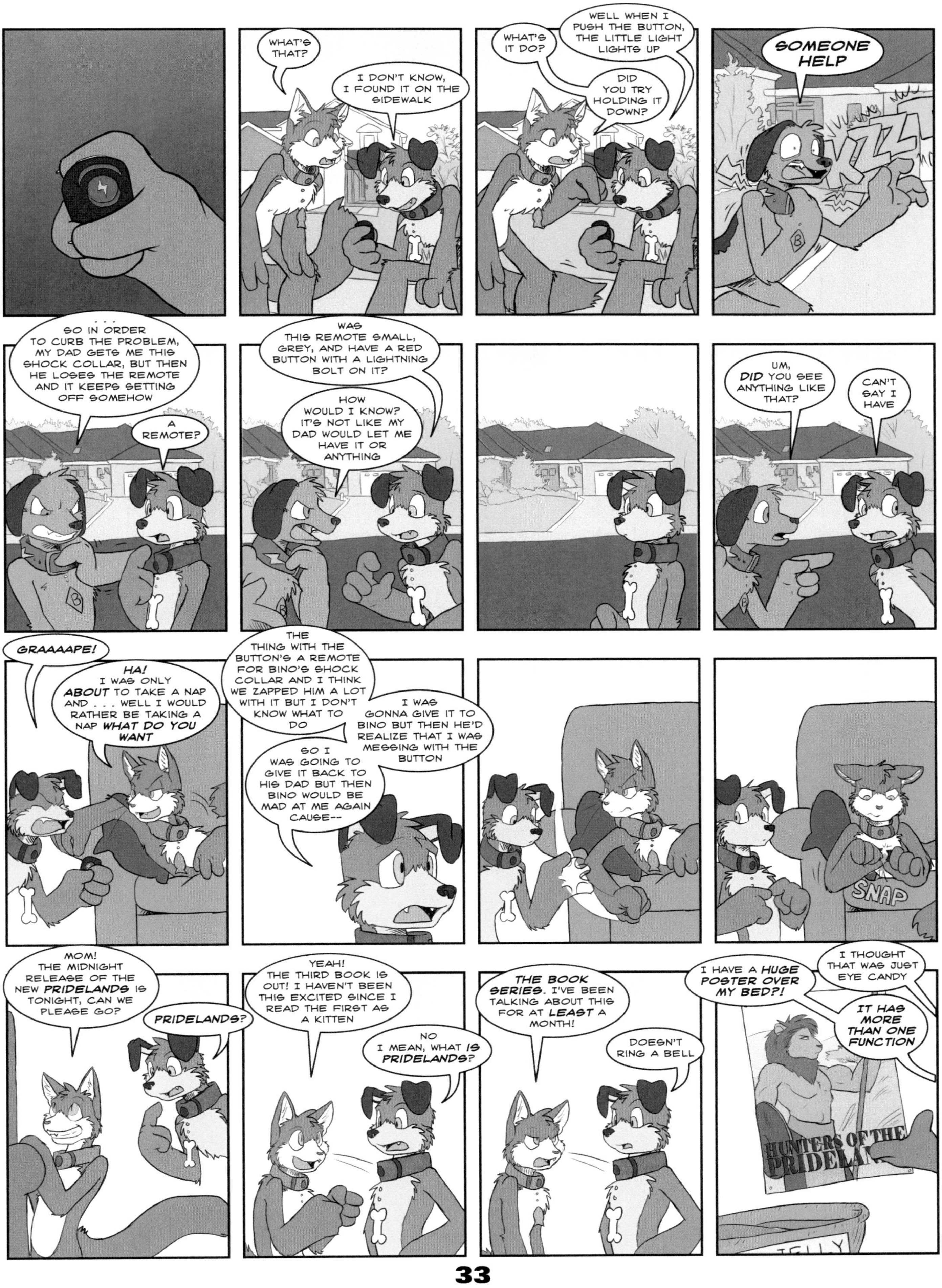
WHAT'S THAT?
I DON'T KNOW, I FOUND IT ON THE SIDEWALK
WHAT'S IT DO?
WELL WHEN I PUSH THE BUTTON, THE LITTLE LIGHT LIGHTS UP
DID YOU TRY HOLDING IT DOWN?
SOMEONE HELP
VZZT
. . . SO IN ORDER TO CURB THE PROBLEM, MY DAD GETS ME THIS SHOCK COLLAR, BUT THEN HE LOSES THE REMOTE AND IT KEEPS SETTING OFF SOMEHOW
A REMOTE?
WAS THIS REMOTE SMALL, GREY, AND HAVE A RED BUTTON WITH A LIGHTNING BOLT ON IT?
HOW WOULD I KNOW? IT'S NOT LIKE MY DAD WOULD LET ME HAVE IT OR ANYTHING
UM, DID YOU SEE ANYTHING LIKE THAT?
CAN'T SAY I HAVE
GRAAAAPE!
HA! I WAS ONLY ABOUT TO TAKE A NAP AND . . . WELL I WOULD RATHER BE TAKING A NAP WHAT DO YOU WANT
THE THING WITH THE BUTTON'S A REMOTE FOR BINO'S SHOCK COLLAR AND I THINK WE ZAPPED HIM A LOT WITH IT BUT I DON'T KNOW WHAT TO DO
I WAS GONNA GIVE IT TO BINO BUT THEN HE'D REALIZE THAT I WAS MESSING WITH THE BUTTON
SO I WAS GOING TO GIVE IT BACK TO HIS DAD BUT THEN BINO WOULD BE MAD AT ME AGAIN CAUSE--
SNAP
MOM! THE MIDNIGHT RELEASE OF THE NEW PRIDELANDS IS TONIGHT, CAN WE PLEASE GO?
PRIDELANDS?
YEAH! THE THIRD BOOK IS OUT! I HAVEN'T BEEN THIS EXCITED SINCE I READ THE FIRST AS A KITTEN
NO I MEAN, WHAT IS PRIDELANDS?
THE BOOK SERIES. I'VE BEEN TALKING ABOUT THIS FOR AT LEAST A MONTH!
DOESN'T RING A BELL
I HAVE A HUGE POSTER OVER MY BED?!
I THOUGHT THAT WAS JUST EYE CANDY
IT HAS MORE THAN ONE FUNCTION
HUNTERS OF THE PRIDELAN

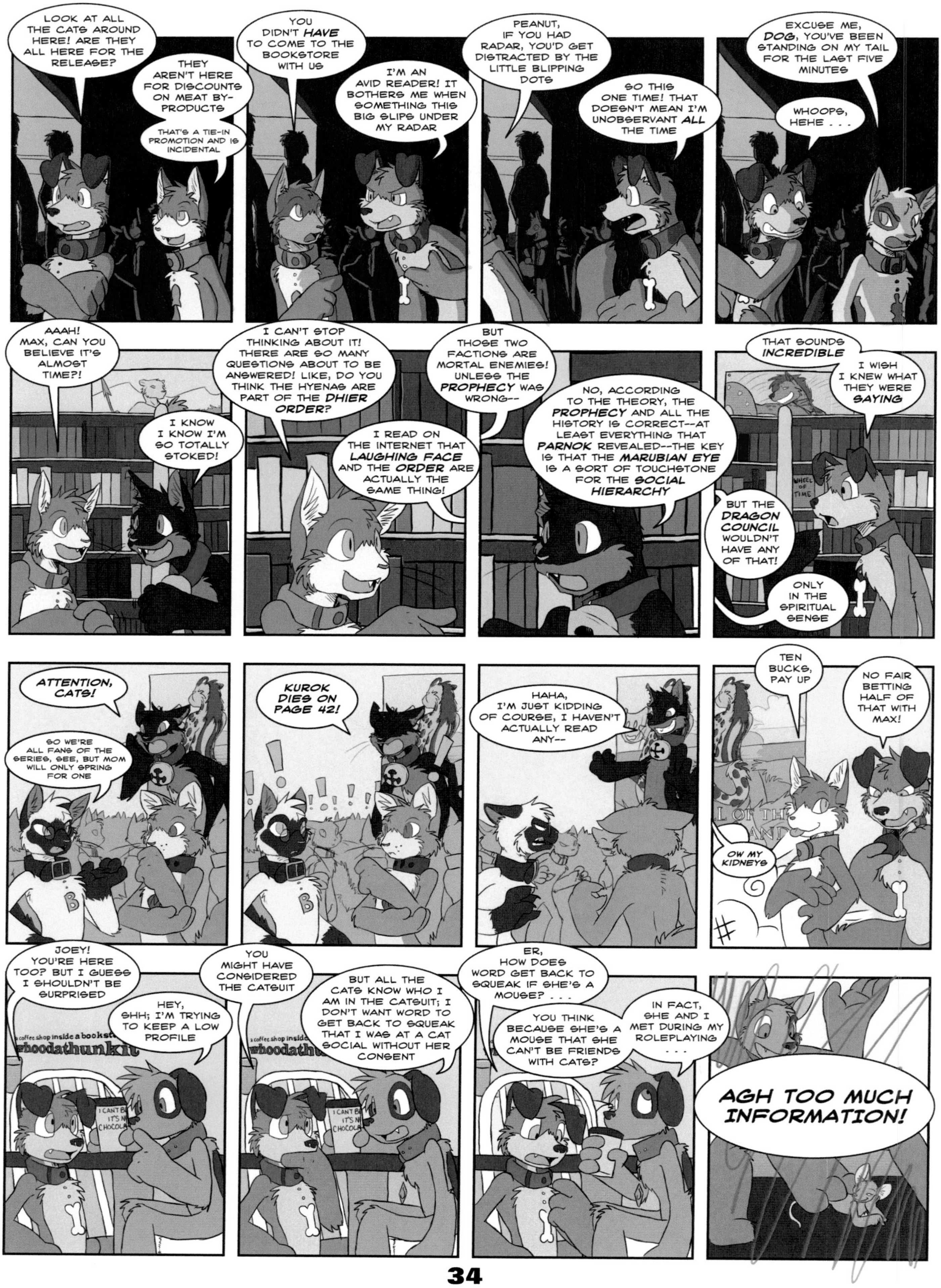
LOOK AT ALL THE CATS AROUND HERE! ARE THEY ALL HERE FOR THE RELEASE?
THEY AREN'T HERE FOR DISCOUNTS ON MEAT BY-PRODUCTS
THAT'S A TIE-IN PROMOTION AND IS INCIDENTAL
YOU DIDN'T HAVE TO COME TO THE BOOKSTORE WITH US
I'M AN AVID READER! IT BOTHERS ME WHEN SOMETHING THIS BIG SLIPS UNDER MY RADAR
PEANUT, IF YOU HAD RADAR, YOU'D GET DISTRACTED BY THE LITTLE BLIPPING DOTS
SO THIS ONE TIME! THAT DOESN'T MEAN I'M UNOBSERVANT ALL THE TIME
EXCUSE ME, DOG, YOU'VE BEEN STANDING ON MY TAIL FOR THE LAST FIVE MINUTES
WHOOPS, HEHE . . .
AAAH! MAX, CAN YOU BELIEVE IT'S ALMOST TIME?!
I KNOW I KNOW I'M SO TOTALLY STOKED!
I CAN'T STOP THINKING ABOUT IT! THERE ARE SO MANY QUESTIONS ABOUT TO BE ANSWERED! LIKE, DO YOU THINK THE HYENAS ARE PART OF THE DHIER ORDER?
I READ ON THE INTERNET THAT LAUGHING FACE AND THE ORDER ARE ACTUALLY THE SAME THING!
BUT THOSE TWO FACTIONS ARE MORTAL ENEMIES! UNLESS THE PROPHECY WAS WRONG--
NO, ACCORDING TO THE THEORY, THE PROPHECY AND ALL THE HISTORY IS CORRECT--AT LEAST EVERYTHING THAT PARNOK REVEALED--THE KEY IS THAT THE MARUBIAN EYE IS A SORT OF TOUCHSTONE FOR THE SOCIAL HIERARCHY
THAT SOUNDS INCREDIBLE
I WISH I KNEW WHAT THEY WERE SAYING
WHEEL OF TIME
BUT THE DRAGON COUNCIL WOULDN'T HAVE ANY OF THAT!
ONLY IN THE SPIRITUAL SENSE
ATTENTION, CATS!
SO WE'RE ALL FANS OF THE SERIES, SEE, BUT MOM WILL ONLY SPRING FOR ONE
KUROK DIES ON PAGE 42!
HAHA, I'M JUST KIDDING OF COURSE, I HAVEN'T ACTUALLY READ ANY--
TEN BUCKS, PAY UP
NO FAIR BETTING HALF OF THAT WITH MAX!
OW MY KIDNEYS
JOEY! YOU'RE HERE TOO? BUT I GUESS I SHOULDN'T BE SURPRISED
HEY, SHH; I'M TRYING TO KEEP A LOW PROFILE
a coffee shop inside a bookst
whoodathunkit
YOU MIGHT HAVE CONSIDERED THE CATSUIT
BUT ALL THE CATS KNOW WHO I AM IN THE CATSUIT; I DON'T WANT WORD TO GET BACK TO SQUEAK THAT I WAS AT A CAT SOCIAL WITHOUT HER CONSENT
ER, HOW DOES WORD GET BACK TO SQUEAK IF SHE'S A MOUSE? . . .
YOU THINK BECAUSE SHE'S A MOUSE THAT SHE CAN'T BE FRIENDS WITH CATS?
IN FACT, SHE AND I MET DURING MY ROLEPLAYING . . .
AGH TOO MUCH INFORMATION!

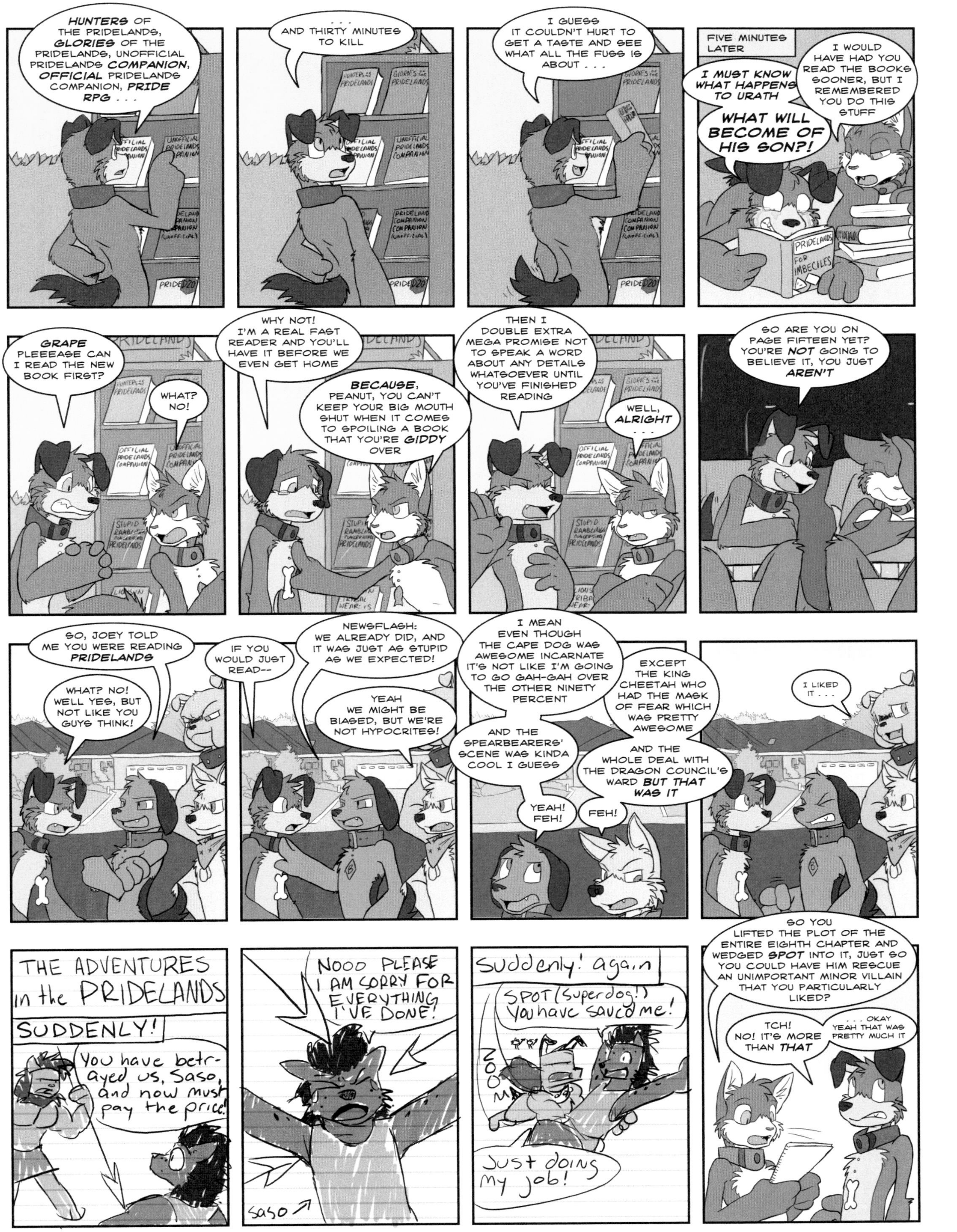
HUNTERS OF THE PRIDELANDS, GLORIES OF THE PRIDELANDS, UNOFFICIAL PRIDELANDS COMPANION, OFFICIAL PRIDELANDS COMPANION, PRIDE RPG . . .
. . . AND THIRTY MINUTES TO KILL
I GUESS IT COULDN'T HURT TO GET A TASTE AND SEE WHAT ALL THE FUSS IS ABOUT . . .
FIVE MINUTES LATER
I MUST KNOW WHAT HAPPENS TO URATH
WHAT WILL BECOME OF HIS SON?!
I WOULD HAVE HAD YOU READ THE BOOKS SOONER, BUT I REMEMBERED YOU DO THIS STUFF
PRIDELANDS FOR IMBECILES
GRAPE PLEEEASE CAN I READ THE NEW BOOK FIRST?
WHAT? NO!
WHY NOT! I'M A REAL FAST READER AND YOU'LL HAVE IT BEFORE WE EVEN GET HOME
BECAUSE, PEANUT, YOU CAN'T KEEP YOUR BIG MOUTH SHUT WHEN IT COMES TO SPOILING A BOOK THAT YOU'RE GIDDY OVER
THEN I DOUBLE EXTRA MEGA PROMISE NOT TO SPEAK A WORD ABOUT ANY DETAILS WHATSOEVER UNTIL YOU'VE FINISHED READING
WELL, ALRIGHT . . .
SO ARE YOU ON PAGE FIFTEEN YET? YOU'RE NOT GOING TO BELIEVE IT, YOU JUST AREN'T
SO, JOEY TOLD ME YOU WERE READING PRIDELANDS
WHAT? NO! WELL YES, BUT NOT LIKE YOU GUYS THINK!
IF YOU WOULD JUST READ--
NEWSFLASH: WE ALREADY DID, AND IT WAS JUST AS STUPID AS WE EXPECTED!
YEAH WE MIGHT BE BIASED, BUT WE'RE NOT HYPOCRITES!
I MEAN EVEN THOUGH THE CAPE DOG WAS AWESOME INCARNATE IT'S NOT LIKE I'M GOING TO GO GAH-GAH OVER THE OTHER NINETY PERCENT
EXCEPT THE KING CHEETAH WHO HAD THE MASK OF FEAR WHICH WAS PRETTY AWESOME
AND THE SPEARBEARERS' SCENE WAS KINDA COOL I GUESS
AND THE WHOLE DEAL WITH THE DRAGON COUNCIL'S WARD BUT THAT WAS IT
YEAH! FEH!
FEH!
I LIKED IT . . .
THE ADVENTURES in the PRIDELANDS
SUDDENLY!
You have betr-ayed us, Saso, and now must pay the price!
NOOO PLEASE I AM SORRY FOR EVERYTHING I'VE DONE!
saso
Suddenly! again
SPOT (Superdog!) You have saved me!
ZOOM
Just doing my job!
SO YOU LIFTED THE PLOT OF THE ENTIRE EIGHTH CHAPTER AND WEDGED SPOT INTO IT, JUST SO YOU COULD HAVE HIM RESCUE AN UNIMPORTANT MINOR VILLAIN THAT YOU PARTICULARLY LIKED?
TCH! NO! IT'S MORE THAN THAT
. . . OKAY YEAH THAT WAS PRETTY MUCH IT

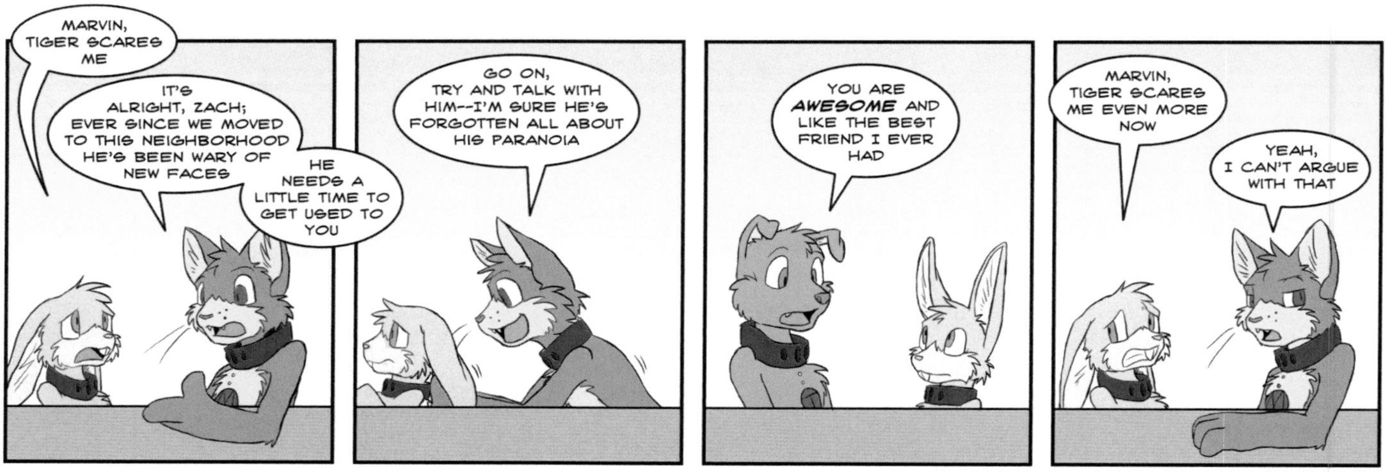
MARVIN, TIGER SCARES ME
IT'S ALRIGHT, ZACH; EVER SINCE WE MOVED TO THIS NEIGHBORHOOD HE'S BEEN WARY OF NEW FACES
HE NEEDS A LITTLE TIME TO GET USED TO YOU
GO ON, TRY AND TALK WITH HIM--I'M SURE HE'S FORGOTTEN ALL ABOUT HIS PARANOIA
YOU ARE **AWESOME** AND LIKE THE BEST FRIEND I EVER HAD
MARVIN, TIGER SCARES ME EVEN MORE NOW
YEAH, I CAN'T ARGUE WITH THAT

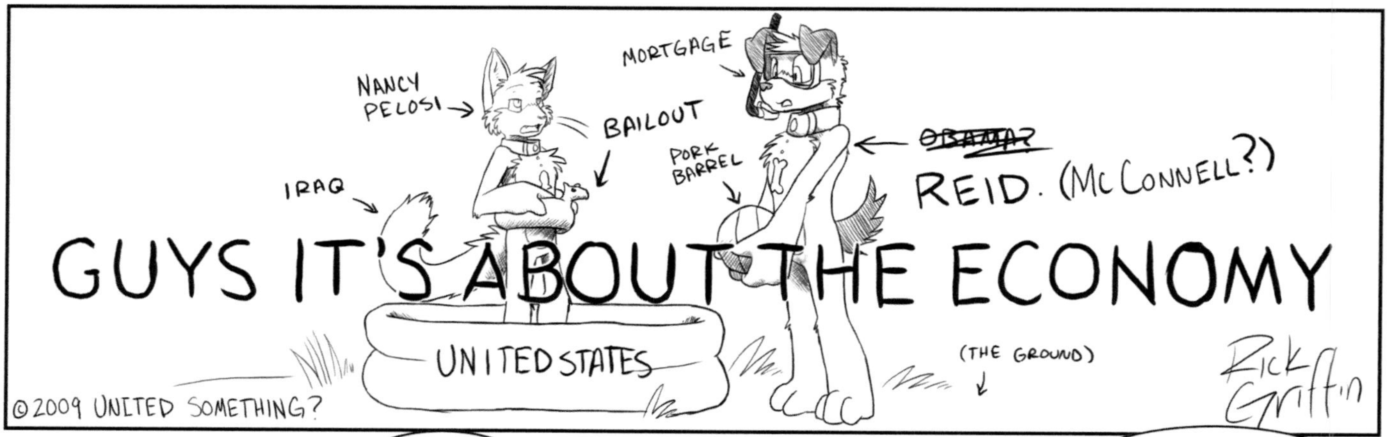
MORTGAGE
NANCY PELOSI
BAILOUT
PORK BARREL
~~OBAMA?~~
REID. (McCONNELL?)
IRAQ
GUYS IT'S ABOUT THE ECONOMY
UNITED STATES
(THE GROUND)
©2009 UNITED SOMETHING?
Rick Griffin

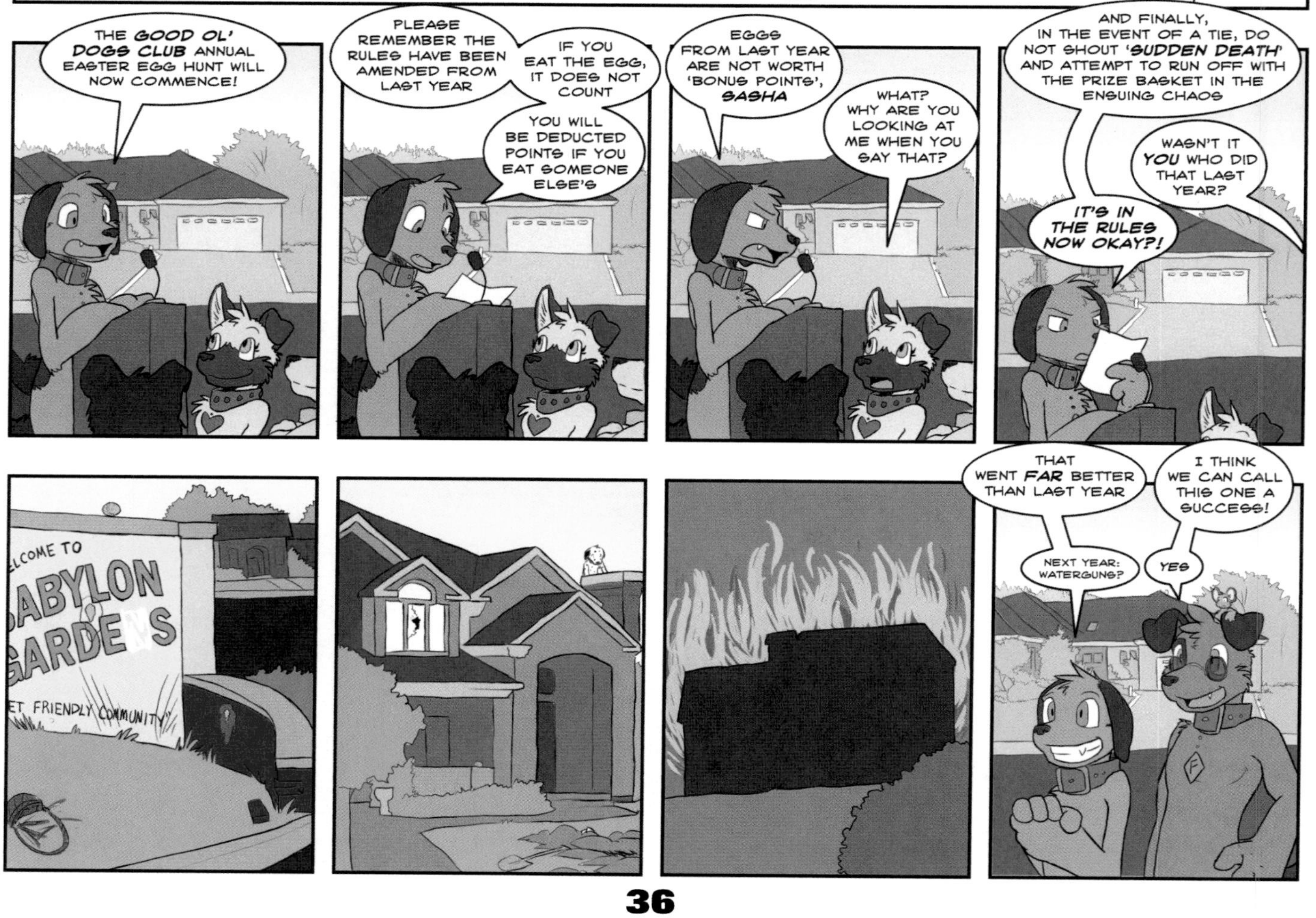
THE ***GOOD OL' DOGS CLUB*** ANNUAL EASTER EGG HUNT WILL NOW COMMENCE!
PLEASE REMEMBER THE RULES HAVE BEEN AMENDED FROM LAST YEAR
IF YOU EAT THE EGG, IT DOES NOT COUNT
YOU WILL BE DEDUCTED POINTS IF YOU EAT SOMEONE ELSE'S
EGGS FROM LAST YEAR ARE NOT WORTH 'BONUS POINTS', ***SASHA***
WHAT? WHY ARE YOU LOOKING AT ME WHEN YOU SAY THAT?
AND FINALLY, IN THE EVENT OF A TIE, DO NOT SHOUT '***SUDDEN DEATH***' AND ATTEMPT TO RUN OFF WITH THE PRIZE BASKET IN THE ENSUING CHAOS
WASN'T IT ***YOU*** WHO DID THAT LAST YEAR?
IT'S IN THE RULES NOW OKAY?!
ELCOME TO
ABYLON
GARDENS
ET FRIENDLY COMMUNITY
THAT WENT ***FAR*** BETTER THAN LAST YEAR
I THINK WE CAN CALL THIS ONE A SUCCESS!
NEXT YEAR: WATERGUNS?
YES

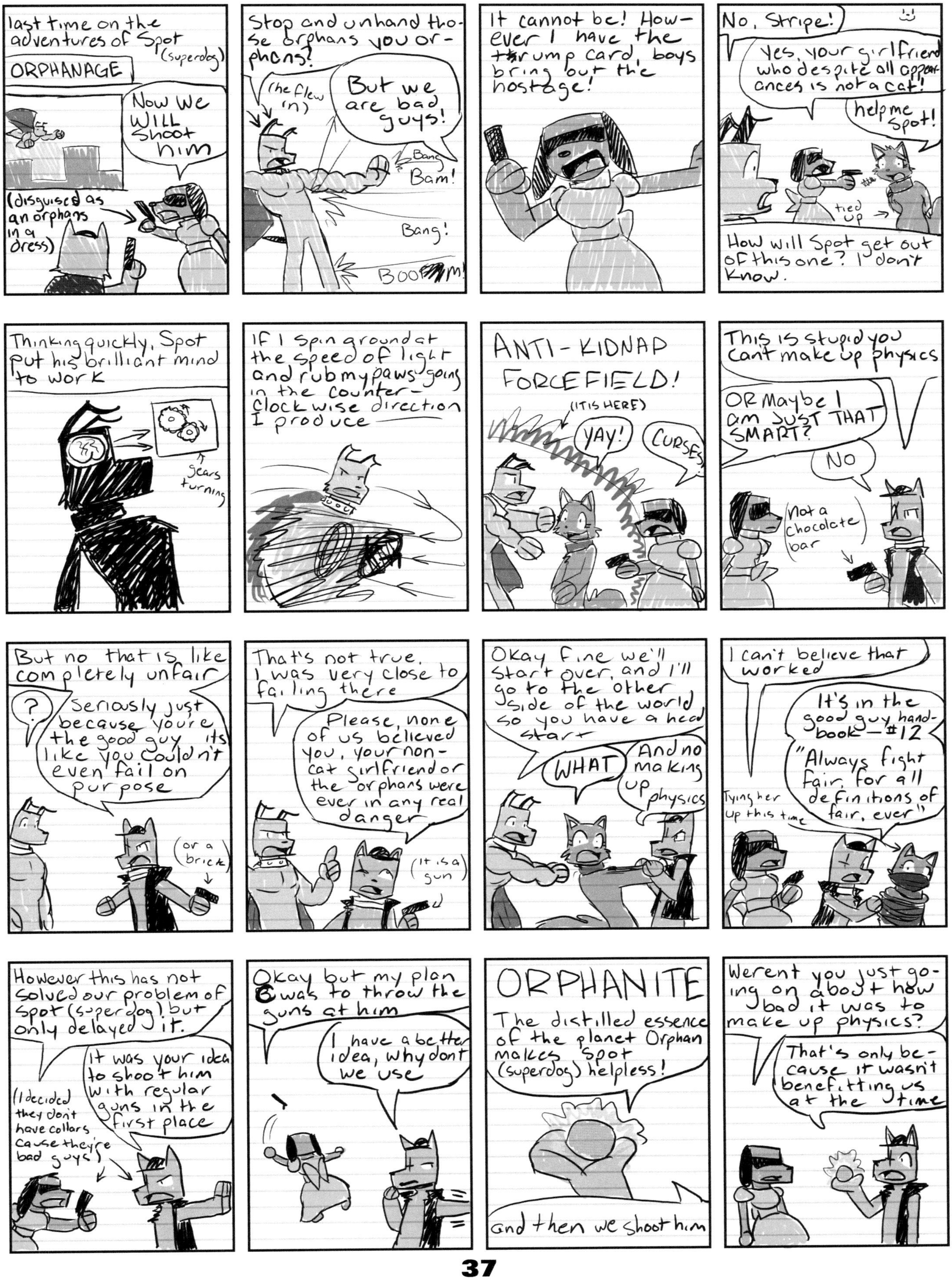
last time on the adventures of Spot (superdog)
ORPHANAGE
Now we will shoot him
(disguised as an orphans in a dress)
Stop and unhand those orphans you orphans?
(he flew in)
But we are bad guys!
Bang
Bam!
Bang!
BOOM!
It cannot be! However I have the trump card, boys bring out the hostage!
No, Stripe!
Yes, your girlfriend who despite all appearances is not a cat!
help me Spot!
tied up
How will Spot get out of this one? I don't know.
Thinking quickly, Spot put his brilliant mind to work
gears turning
If I spin around at the speed of light and rub my paws going in the counter-clockwise direction I produce
ANTI-KIDNAP FORCEFIELD!
(IT IS HERE)
YAY!
CURSES
This is stupid you cant make up physics
OR Maybe I am JUST THAT SMART?
NO
(Not a chocolate bar
But no that is like completely unfair
?
Seriously just because you're the good guy its like you couldn't even fail on purpose
(or a brick)
That's not true. I was very close to failing there
Please, none of us believed you, your non-cat girlfriend or the orphans were ever in any real danger
(It is a gun
Okay fine we'll start over, and I'll go to the other side of the world so you have a head start
WHAT
And no making up physics
I can't believe that worked
It's in the good guy handbook — #12
"Always fight fair, for all definitions of fair, ever"
Tying her up this time
However this has not solved our problem of Spot (superdog) but only delayed it.
It was your idea to shoot him with regular guns in the first place
(I decided they don't have collars cause they're bad guys)
Okay but my plan was to throw the guns at him
I have a better idea, why dont we use
ORPHANITE
The distilled essence of the planet Orphan makes Spot (superdog) helpless!
and then we shoot him
Werent you just going on about how bad it was to make up physics?
That's only because it wasn't benefitting us at the time

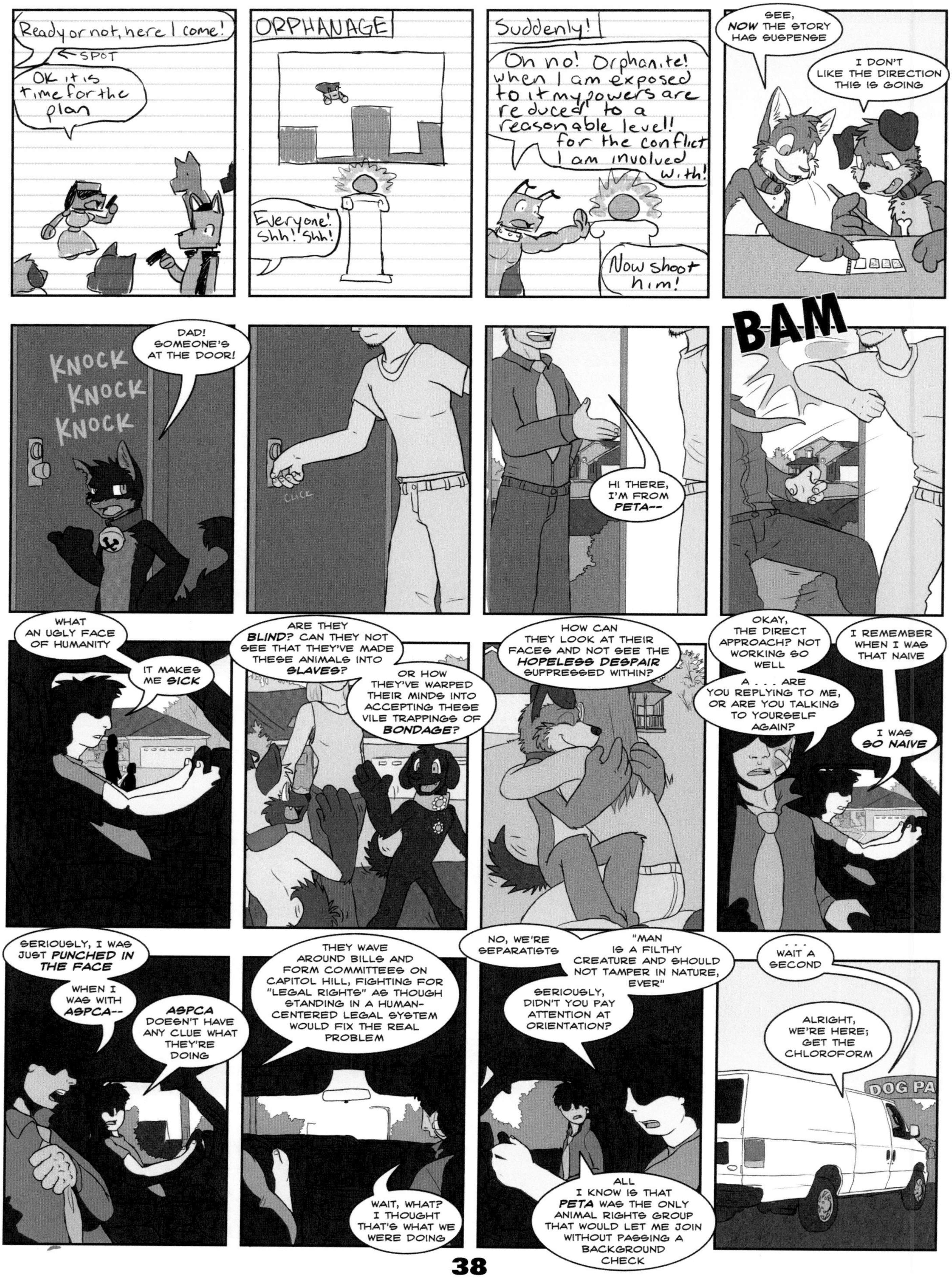
Ready or not, here I come!
SPOT
OK it is time for the plan
ORPHANAGE
Everyone! Shh! Shh!
Suddenly!
On no! Orphanite! when I am exposed to it my powers are reduced to a reasonable level! for the conflict I am involved with!
Now shoot him!
SEE, NOW THE STORY HAS SUSPENSE
I DON'T LIKE THE DIRECTION THIS IS GOING
KNOCK KNOCK KNOCK
DAD! SOMEONE'S AT THE DOOR!
CLICK
HI THERE, I'M FROM PETA--
BAM
WHAT AN UGLY FACE OF HUMANITY
IT MAKES ME SICK
ARE THEY BLIND? CAN THEY NOT SEE THAT THEY'VE MADE THESE ANIMALS INTO SLAVES?
OR HOW THEY'VE WARPED THEIR MINDS INTO ACCEPTING THESE VILE TRAPPINGS OF BONDAGE?
HOW CAN THEY LOOK AT THEIR FACES AND NOT SEE THE HOPELESS DESPAIR SUPPRESSED WITHIN?
OKAY, THE DIRECT APPROACH? NOT WORKING SO WELL
I REMEMBER WHEN I WAS THAT NAIVE
A . . . ARE YOU REPLYING TO ME, OR ARE YOU TALKING TO YOURSELF AGAIN?
I WAS SO NAIVE
SERIOUSLY, I WAS JUST PUNCHED IN THE FACE
WHEN I WAS WITH ASPCA--
ASPCA DOESN'T HAVE ANY CLUE WHAT THEY'RE DOING
THEY WAVE AROUND BILLS AND FORM COMMITTEES ON CAPITOL HILL, FIGHTING FOR "LEGAL RIGHTS" AS THOUGH STANDING IN A HUMAN-CENTERED LEGAL SYSTEM WOULD FIX THE REAL PROBLEM
WAIT, WHAT? I THOUGHT THAT'S WHAT WE WERE DOING
NO, WE'RE SEPARATISTS
"MAN IS A FILTHY CREATURE AND SHOULD NOT TAMPER IN NATURE, EVER"
SERIOUSLY, DIDN'T YOU PAY ATTENTION AT ORIENTATION?
ALL I KNOW IS THAT PETA WAS THE ONLY ANIMAL RIGHTS GROUP THAT WOULD LET ME JOIN WITHOUT PASSING A BACKGROUND CHECK
. . . WAIT A SECOND
ALRIGHT, WE'RE HERE; GET THE CHLOROFORM
DOG PA

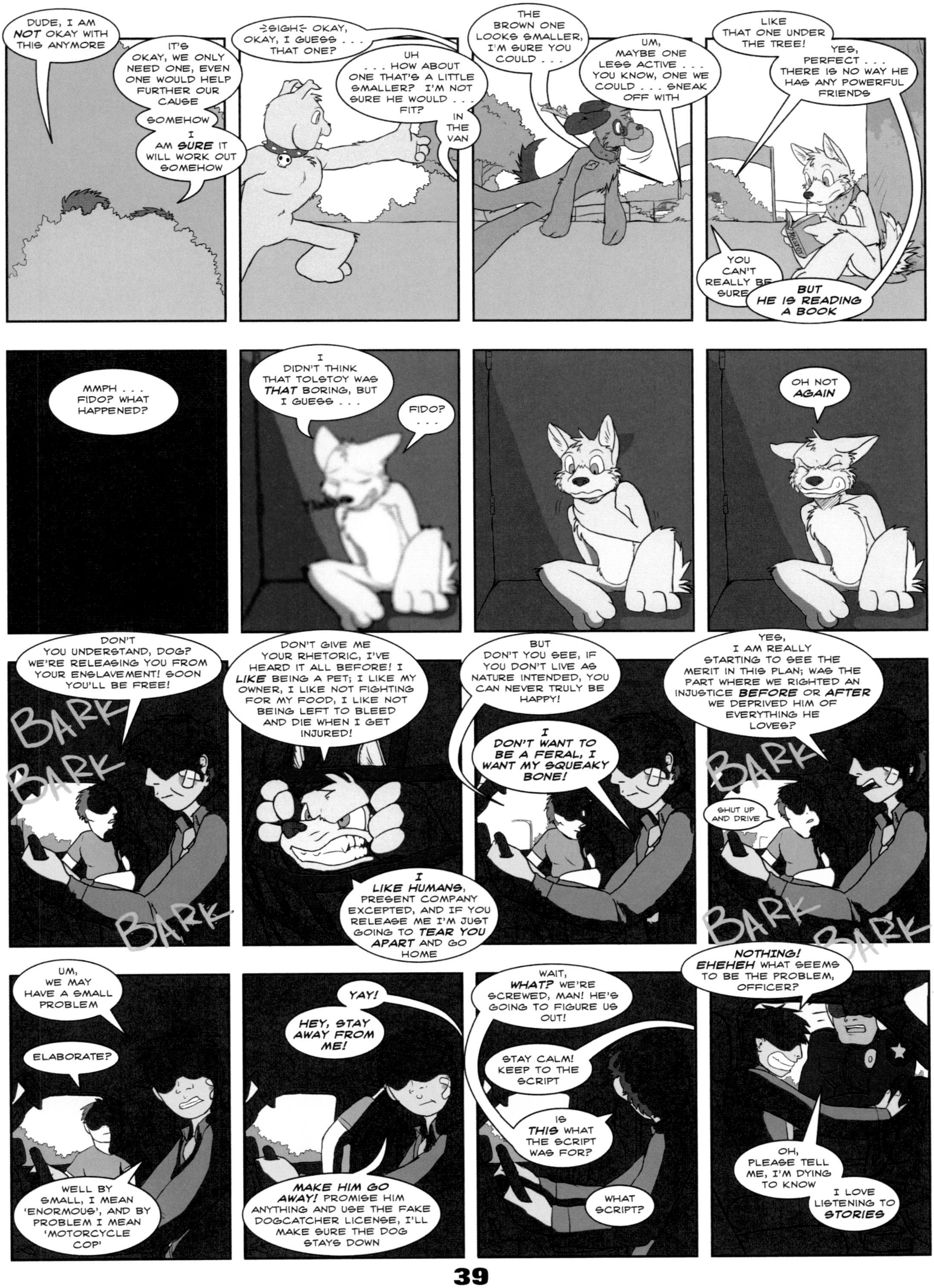
DUDE, I AM NOT OKAY WITH THIS ANYMORE
IT'S OKAY, WE ONLY NEED ONE, EVEN ONE WOULD HELP FURTHER OUR CAUSE
SOMEHOW
I AM SURE IT WILL WORK OUT SOMEHOW
-SIGH- OKAY, OKAY, I GUESS . . . THAT ONE?
UH . . . HOW ABOUT ONE THAT'S A LITTLE SMALLER? I'M NOT SURE HE WOULD . . . FIT?
IN THE VAN
THE BROWN ONE LOOKS SMALLER, I'M SURE YOU COULD . . .
UM, MAYBE ONE LESS ACTIVE . . . YOU KNOW, ONE WE COULD . . . SNEAK OFF WITH
LIKE THAT ONE UNDER THE TREE!
YES, PERFECT . . . THERE IS NO WAY HE HAS ANY POWERFUL FRIENDS
YOU CAN'T REALLY BE SURE
BUT HE IS READING A BOOK
MMPH . . . FIDO? WHAT HAPPENED?
I DIDN'T THINK THAT TOLSTOY WAS THAT BORING, BUT I GUESS . . .
FIDO? . . .
OH NOT AGAIN
DON'T YOU UNDERSTAND, DOG? WE'RE RELEASING YOU FROM YOUR ENSLAVEMENT! SOON YOU'LL BE FREE!
BARK
BARK
BARK
DON'T GIVE ME YOUR RHETORIC, I'VE HEARD IT ALL BEFORE! I LIKE BEING A PET; I LIKE MY OWNER, I LIKE NOT FIGHTING FOR MY FOOD, I LIKE NOT BEING LEFT TO BLEED AND DIE WHEN I GET INJURED!
I LIKE HUMANS, PRESENT COMPANY EXCEPTED, AND IF YOU RELEASE ME I'M JUST GOING TO TEAR YOU APART AND GO HOME
BUT DON'T YOU SEE, IF YOU DON'T LIVE AS NATURE INTENDED, YOU CAN NEVER TRULY BE HAPPY!
I DON'T WANT TO BE A FERAL, I WANT MY SQUEAKY BONE!
YES, I AM REALLY STARTING TO SEE THE MERIT IN THIS PLAN; WAS THE PART WHERE WE RIGHTED AN INJUSTICE BEFORE OR AFTER WE DEPRIVED HIM OF EVERYTHING HE LOVES?
SHUT UP AND DRIVE
BARK
BARK
BARK
UM, WE MAY HAVE A SMALL PROBLEM
ELABORATE?
WELL BY SMALL, I MEAN 'ENORMOUS', AND BY PROBLEM I MEAN 'MOTORCYCLE COP'
YAY!
HEY, STAY AWAY FROM ME!
MAKE HIM GO AWAY! PROMISE HIM ANYTHING AND USE THE FAKE DOGCATCHER LICENSE, I'LL MAKE SURE THE DOG STAYS DOWN
WAIT, WHAT? WE'RE SCREWED, MAN! HE'S GOING TO FIGURE US OUT!
STAY CALM! KEEP TO THE SCRIPT
IS THIS WHAT THE SCRIPT WAS FOR?
WHAT SCRIPT?
NOTHING! EHEHEH WHAT SEEMS TO BE THE PROBLEM, OFFICER?
OH, PLEASE TELL ME, I'M DYING TO KNOW
I LOVE LISTENING TO STORIES

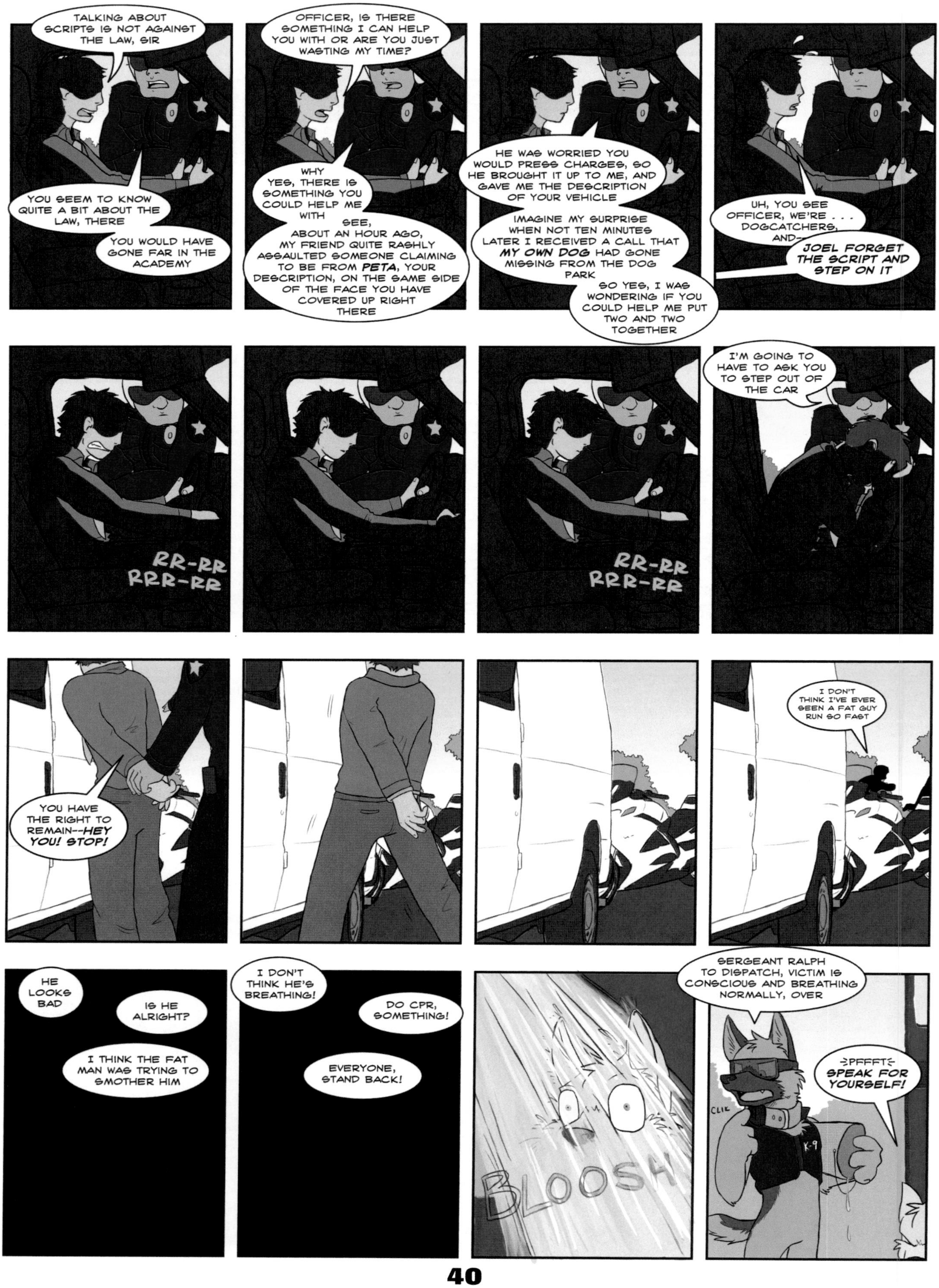
TALKING ABOUT SCRIPTS IS NOT AGAINST THE LAW, SIR
YOU SEEM TO KNOW QUITE A BIT ABOUT THE LAW, THERE
YOU WOULD HAVE GONE FAR IN THE ACADEMY
OFFICER, IS THERE SOMETHING I CAN HELP YOU WITH OR ARE YOU JUST WASTING MY TIME?
WHY YES, THERE IS SOMETHING YOU COULD HELP ME WITH
SEE, ABOUT AN HOUR AGO, MY FRIEND QUITE RASHLY ASSAULTED SOMEONE CLAIMING TO BE FROM PETA, YOUR DESCRIPTION, ON THE SAME SIDE OF THE FACE YOU HAVE COVERED UP RIGHT THERE
HE WAS WORRIED YOU WOULD PRESS CHARGES, SO HE BROUGHT IT UP TO ME, AND GAVE ME THE DESCRIPTION OF YOUR VEHICLE
IMAGINE MY SURPRISE WHEN NOT TEN MINUTES LATER I RECEIVED A CALL THAT MY OWN DOG HAD GONE MISSING FROM THE DOG PARK
SO YES, I WAS WONDERING IF YOU COULD HELP ME PUT TWO AND TWO TOGETHER
UH, YOU SEE OFFICER, WE'RE . . . DOGCATCHERS, AND—
JOEL FORGET THE SCRIPT AND STEP ON IT
RR-RR RRR-RR
RR-RR RRR-RR
I'M GOING TO HAVE TO ASK YOU TO STEP OUT OF THE CAR
YOU HAVE THE RIGHT TO REMAIN--HEY YOU! STOP!
I DON'T THINK I'VE EVER SEEN A FAT GUY RUN SO FAST
HE LOOKS BAD
IS HE ALRIGHT?
I THINK THE FAT MAN WAS TRYING TO SMOTHER HIM
I DON'T THINK HE'S BREATHING!
DO CPR, SOMETHING!
EVERYONE, STAND BACK!
BLOOSH
SERGEANT RALPH TO DISPATCH, VICTIM IS CONSCIOUS AND BREATHING NORMALLY, OVER
CLIK
K-9
⇒PFFFT⇐ SPEAK FOR YOURSELF!

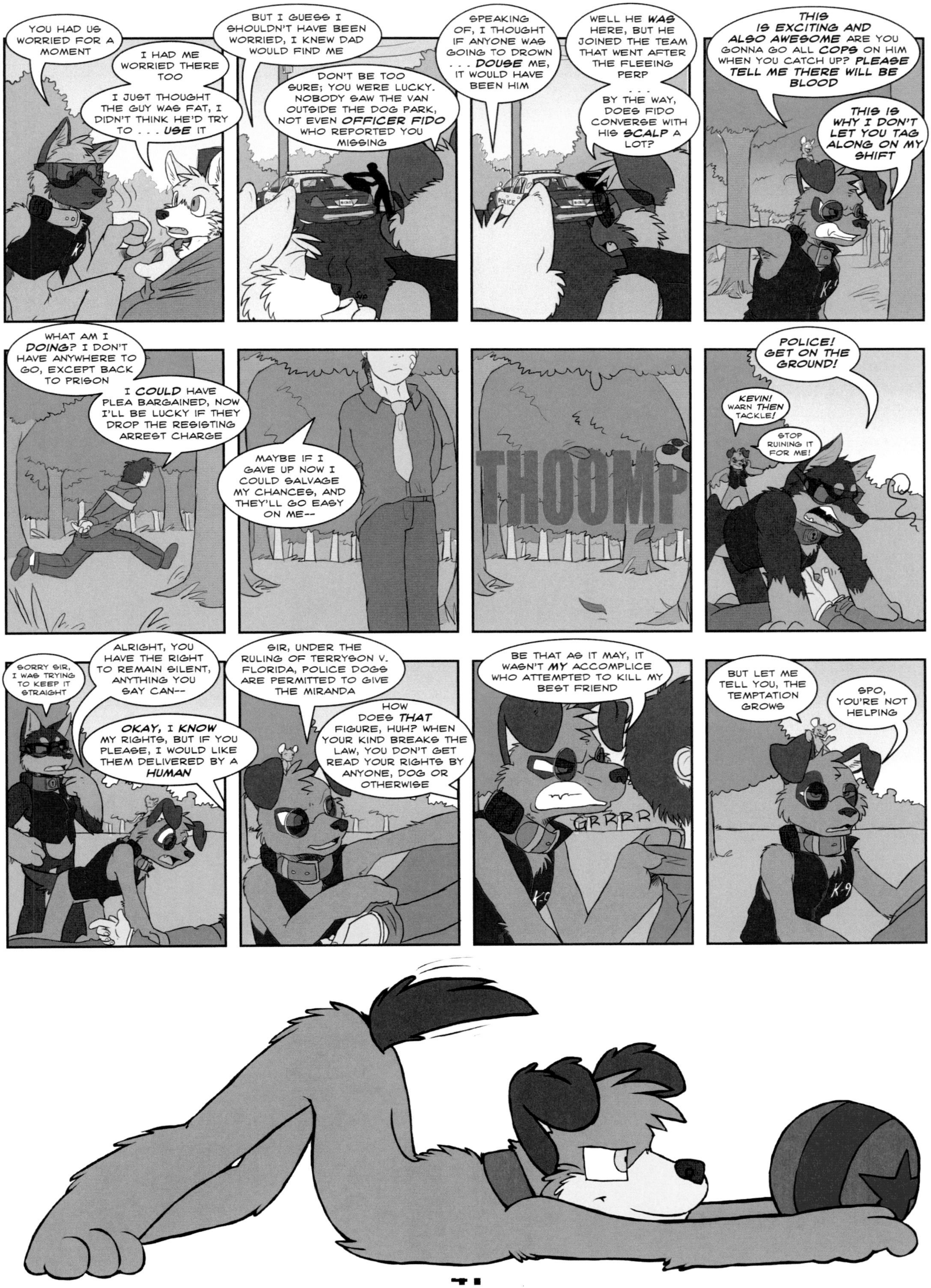
YOU HAD US WORRIED FOR A MOMENT
I HAD ME WORRIED THERE TOO
I JUST THOUGHT THE GUY WAS FAT, I DIDN'T THINK HE'D TRY TO . . . USE IT
BUT I GUESS I SHOULDN'T HAVE BEEN WORRIED, I KNEW DAD WOULD FIND ME
DON'T BE TOO SURE; YOU WERE LUCKY. NOBODY SAW THE VAN OUTSIDE THE DOG PARK, NOT EVEN OFFICER FIDO WHO REPORTED YOU MISSING
SPEAKING OF, I THOUGHT IF ANYONE WAS GOING TO DROWN . . . DOUSE ME, IT WOULD HAVE BEEN HIM
WELL HE WAS HERE, BUT HE JOINED THE TEAM THAT WENT AFTER THE FLEEING PERP
. . .
BY THE WAY, DOES FIDO CONVERSE WITH HIS SCALP A LOT?
THIS IS EXCITING AND ALSO AWESOME ARE YOU GONNA GO ALL COPS ON HIM WHEN YOU CATCH UP? PLEASE TELL ME THERE WILL BE BLOOD
THIS IS WHY I DON'T LET YOU TAG ALONG ON MY SHIFT
WHAT AM I DOING? I DON'T HAVE ANYWHERE TO GO, EXCEPT BACK TO PRISON
I COULD HAVE PLEA BARGAINED, NOW I'LL BE LUCKY IF THEY DROP THE RESISTING ARREST CHARGE
MAYBE IF I GAVE UP NOW I COULD SALVAGE MY CHANCES, AND THEY'LL GO EASY ON ME--
THOOMP
POLICE! GET ON THE GROUND!
KEVIN! WARN THEN TACKLE!
STOP RUINING IT FOR ME!
SORRY SIR, I WAS TRYING TO KEEP IT STRAIGHT
ALRIGHT, YOU HAVE THE RIGHT TO REMAIN SILENT, ANYTHING YOU SAY CAN--
OKAY, I KNOW MY RIGHTS, BUT IF YOU PLEASE, I WOULD LIKE THEM DELIVERED BY A HUMAN
SIR, UNDER THE RULING OF TERRYSON V. FLORIDA, POLICE DOGS ARE PERMITTED TO GIVE THE MIRANDA
HOW DOES THAT FIGURE, HUH? WHEN YOUR KIND BREAKS THE LAW, YOU DON'T GET READ YOUR RIGHTS BY ANYONE, DOG OR OTHERWISE
BE THAT AS IT MAY, IT WASN'T MY ACCOMPLICE WHO ATTEMPTED TO KILL MY BEST FRIEND
GRRRR
BUT LET ME TELL YOU, THE TEMPTATION GROWS
SPO, YOU'RE NOT HELPING

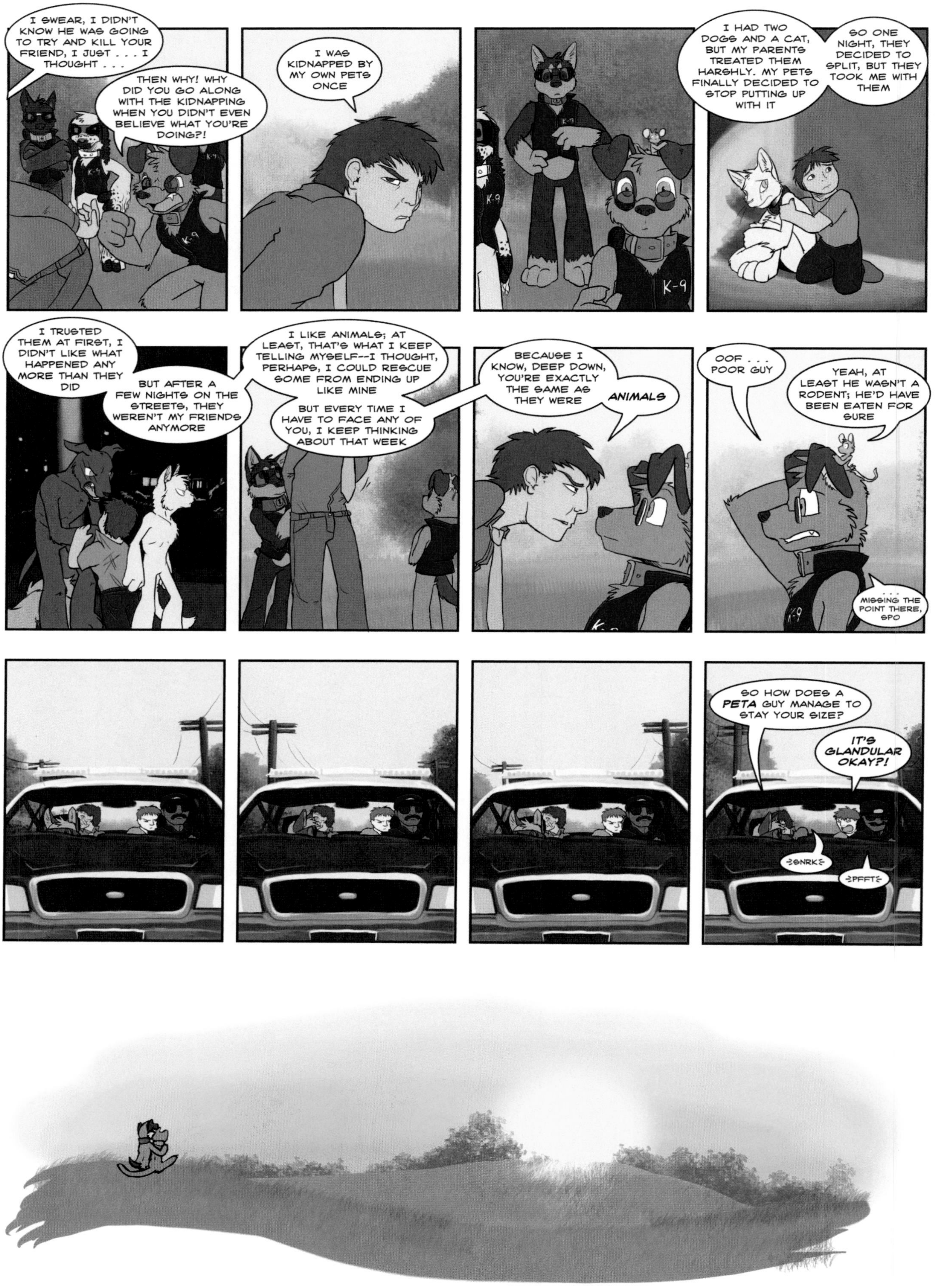
I SWEAR, I DIDN'T KNOW HE WAS GOING TO TRY AND KILL YOUR FRIEND, I JUST . . . I THOUGHT . . .
THEN WHY! WHY DID YOU GO ALONG WITH THE KIDNAPPING WHEN YOU DIDN'T EVEN BELIEVE WHAT YOU'RE DOING?!
I WAS KIDNAPPED BY MY OWN PETS ONCE
I HAD TWO DOGS AND A CAT, BUT MY PARENTS TREATED THEM HARSHLY. MY PETS FINALLY DECIDED TO STOP PUTTING UP WITH IT
SO ONE NIGHT, THEY DECIDED TO SPLIT, BUT THEY TOOK ME WITH THEM
I TRUSTED THEM AT FIRST, I DIDN'T LIKE WHAT HAPPENED ANY MORE THAN THEY DID
BUT AFTER A FEW NIGHTS ON THE STREETS, THEY WEREN'T MY FRIENDS ANYMORE
I LIKE ANIMALS; AT LEAST, THAT'S WHAT I KEEP TELLING MYSELF--I THOUGHT, PERHAPS, I COULD RESCUE SOME FROM ENDING UP LIKE MINE
BUT EVERY TIME I HAVE TO FACE ANY OF YOU, I KEEP THINKING ABOUT THAT WEEK
BECAUSE I KNOW, DEEP DOWN, YOU'RE EXACTLY THE SAME AS THEY WERE
ANIMALS
OOF . . . POOR GUY
YEAH, AT LEAST HE WASN'T A RODENT; HE'D HAVE BEEN EATEN FOR SURE
. . . MISSING THE POINT THERE, SPO
SO HOW DOES A PETA GUY MANAGE TO STAY YOUR SIZE?
IT'S GLANDULAR OKAY?!
SNRK
PFFT

NEXT TIME, ON
HOUSEPETS!

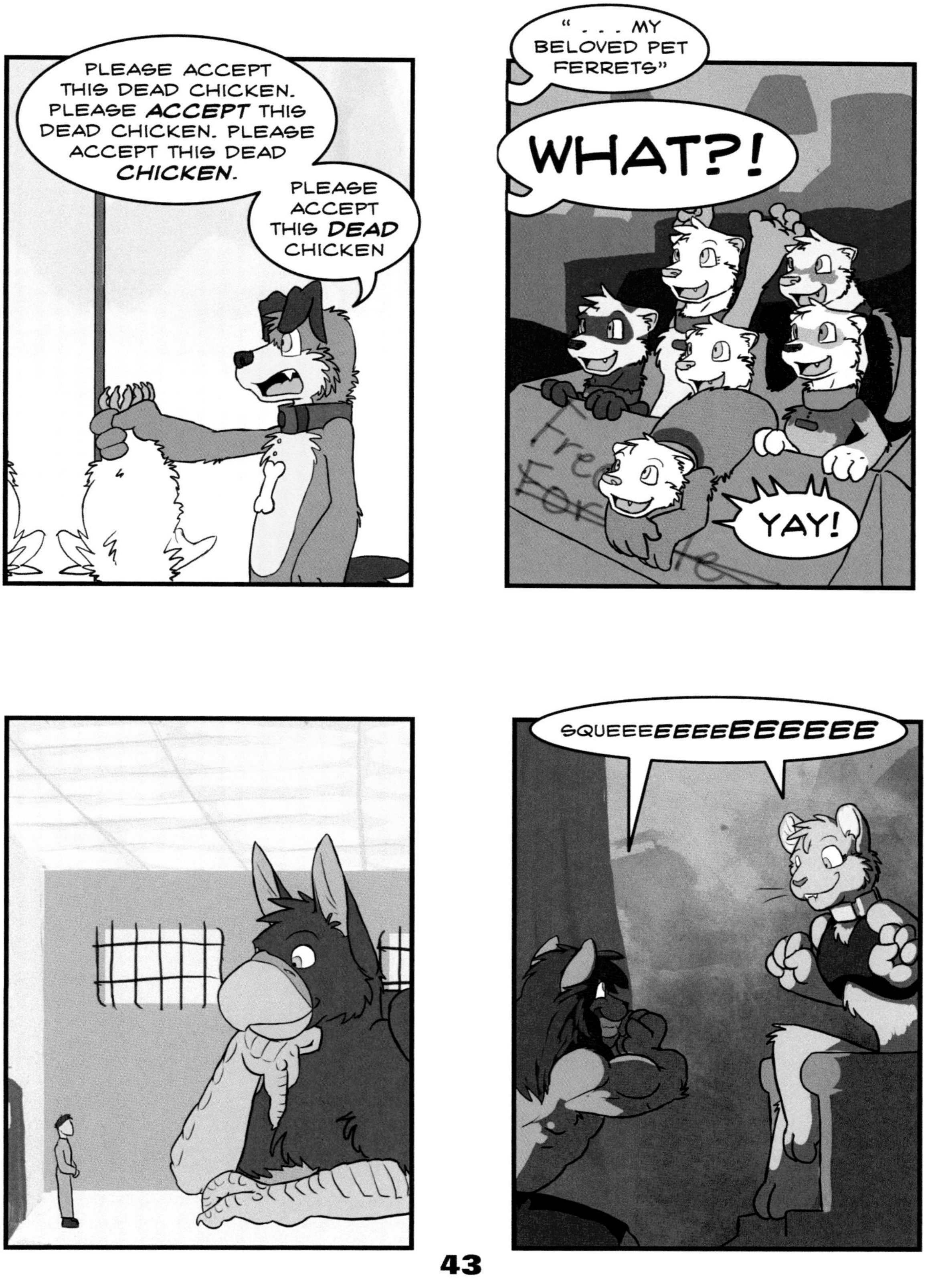

PLEASE ACCEPT THIS DEAD CHICKEN. PLEASE *ACCEPT* THIS DEAD CHICKEN. PLEASE ACCEPT THIS DEAD *CHICKEN*.
PLEASE ACCEPT THIS *DEAD* CHICKEN
“ . . . MY BELOVED PET FERRETS”
WHAT?!
YAY!
SQUEEEEEEEEEEEEEE

Made in the USA
Las Vegas, NV
20 February 2024